"ARE YOU TRYING TO SEDUCE ME?" JIM ASKED.

"Andrea?" He took her by the shoulders, the heat of his talented hands burning through her shirt, and turned her to face him. "Look at me," he ordered softly.

Andie obediently raised her eyes to his.

"Well, I'll be damned," he said when he saw what was in them. "You *are* trying to seduce me."

"What if I am?"

"Well..." One corner of his beautiful mouth turned up in a teasing little smile. "I could protest and say I'm not that kind of guy, but..."

"But?" she whispered, unable to look away.

"We'd both know I was lying through my teeth."

"Well, then...?" She leaned closer, feeling the hardness of his arousal, lusting after his tempting mouth, wanting to demand—or beg—that he make love to her, right now.

"Just one question," he murmured, delaying the inevitable for one deliciously frustrating moment.

Andie sighed and answered in a voice throaty with need. "What?"

"Will you still respect me in the morning?"

She laughed as she reached for him. "I'd say that depends on how well you do tonight."

Candace Schuler is a published author today because years ago her husband, Joe, dared her to use her writing talent to create something other than office memos and computer manuals. Twenty-six books later, she still doesn't know whether to smother him with kisses of gratitude for pointing (okay, pushing!) her in the right direction, or to whack him upside the head for getting her into this crazy business.

Writing is both the most satisfying job she's ever had and the hardest work she's ever done. Often it manages to be both at once. Still, she keeps writing. Mostly because she can't not write. And because—most of the time, anyway—writing manages to be a thoroughly enjoyable way to make a living.

She gets to work at home with her two geriatric cats sleeping in the sun on the window ledge and her dog curled up in a bed next to her desk. She doesn't have to wear boring dress-for-success suits or panty hose, either. And she actually gets paid for telling stories all day. What could be better?

On a more personal note...Candace has been well and truly married for almost twenty-seven years to a wonderful man who knows her better than she knows herself and still loves her, anyway. They've lived all over the country, from a schooner anchored in Oahu's Ala Wai Harbor to a loft in Greenwich Village, New York, with (at last count) fourteen other addresses in between. She currently resides in Minnesota with two outrageously spoiled cats and an eighty-pound Doberman who thinks she's a lapdog.

Look for future titles by Candace in both the Temptation and Blaze series.

Books by Candace Schuler

HARLEQUIN TEMPTATION
553—SEDUCED AND BETRAYED
557—PASSION AND SCANDAL
608—LUCK OF THE DRAW

CANDACE SCHULER
OUT OF CONTROL

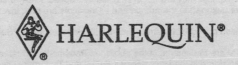

HARLEQUIN®

TORONTO • NEW YORK • LONDON
AMSTERDAM • PARIS • SYDNEY • HAMBURG
STOCKHOLM • ATHENS • TOKYO • MILAN • MADRID
PRAGUE • WARSAW • BUDAPEST • AUCKLAND

ISBN 0-373-51118-3

OUT OF CONTROL

1

THERE WAS GRAFFITI on the wall again, ugly slashes of red paint marring the fresh white plaster and the satiny grain of the walnut paneling below it. It had been nearly a week since the last incident, and Andie had been beginning to hope that the disgruntled artist had finally given up his vendetta against her. But he had apparently only been taking a short break before he turned up the pressure. This latest effort went a step beyond the angry adolescent stage of calling her names and questioning her sexual identity, issuing thinly veiled threats. Be Afraid, Bitch, it said, and for a minute, Andie was.

She glanced around apprehensively, wondering if whoever had vandalized the job site was lurking in one of the empty rooms behind her or in the wide upstairs hall, waiting to give weight to his hateful words with physical force. She was all alone in the rambling old mansion; even the most conscientious of her crew wouldn't start showing up for work for another ten or fifteen minutes. Plenty of time for someone bent on teaching her a lesson about a woman's place to make his point.

And then she dismissed the thought deliberately, through sheer strength of will and the common sense on which she prided herself. Men who wrote nasty slogans on walls seldom had the balls to do more. It was a coward's tactic, meant to frighten and intimidate. Well, Andrea Wagner wouldn't allow herself to be frightened or intimidated. Not by anyone. Not ever again.

It wasn't as if it was the first time something like this had happened to her, and it wouldn't be the last. Certain of her peers in the construction industry didn't like to see a woman succeed at a "man's" job, and they didn't care who knew it. She'd seen and heard it all in the nine years she'd been in the business.

The harassment—some of it good-natured, most of it not—had started the day she'd showed up at the union hall to take the admittance exam for the plumbers' apprenticeship program. She'd been one of only five women in a room full of men, all of them vying for the same few openings. Her practical skills were nonexistent, but she had scored exceptionally high on the math portion of the test, and her aptitude for spatial relations surprised even her. Given her scores, they couldn't, by law, refuse to let her enter the program. But they could try to make her quit. And some of them gave it their best shot.

She'd heard all the rude names, listened to the crude propositions, endured the lewd pinups and the occasional sweaty jock strap in her toolbox. It had been hard at first, and she'd spent more than one night crying into her pillow and wondering if she was doing the right thing. But she had stuck it out. She'd made it through the plumbers' apprenticeship program, adding carpentry and some basic electrical skills to her repertoire along the way, and gone on, finally, to get her journeyman certification. She'd put an ad in the Yellow Pages then and had struck out on her own.

Along the way, she'd toughened up, both mentally

and physically. She wasn't a wet-behind-the-ears rookie anymore, one who blushed at the mildest innuendo, and she'd learned a long time ago that the best way to deal with certain kinds of harassment was to ignore it. She was fully convinced that when the perpetrator of this latest bit of juvenile acting-out behavior realized it wasn't going to have the desired effect, he would stop doing it. Eventually. Making a big deal out of it would only give him what he wanted and prolong the unpleasantness.

With a sigh of resignation and a quick look at the rugged, man-size watch strapped to her wrist, Andie moistened a clean rag with turpentine and carefully began daubing at the red paint. It was still slightly tacky to the touch, making it easy to wipe off of the wooden chair rail and the elegantly carved paneling on the bottom half of the wall. A little buffing with a fine-grade sandpaper and the wood would be as good as new, ready for the next step in refinishing. The wall above it was another story. The paint had soaked deep into the fresh plaster, and the whole upper section would have to be removed and replastered before work could proceed.

The best Andie could do now, before her crew arrived, was to smear the paint around in an effort to make the offensive words less readable. There was no sense in getting everybody riled up over nothing. And it *was* nothing, she reassured herself as she worked. Absolutely nothing.

Still, she jumped like a scalded cat and whirled around with the paint-stained rag clutched in her fist when the front door creaked open behind her. "Good Lord," she said, when she saw who it was. "You nearly scared the life out of me, sneaking up behind me like that."

"I'd hardly call coming in through the front door in broad daylight sneaking," her sister objected mildly as she set her briefcase on a flat section of the scaffolding that climbed up the soaring, two-story wall of the foyer. "That brick walkway out front echoes every step." She flipped open the locks of the briefcase with her thumbs and lifted the lid. "Anyway, even without bricks, you can't sneak in high heels. It's a physical impossibil—" The look in Natalie's soft brown eyes sharpened behind the lenses of her stylish tortoiseshell glasses. "Graffiti?" she said, staring at the words smeared across the wall. "What did it say this time?"

"The usual." Andie shrugged nonchalantly and moved away from the wall, head down as she wiped at her palms with the paint-smeared rag. What she wanted to do was turn around and make sure the words had been completely obliterated, but that would only focus her sister's attention on them. And Natalie was like a pit bull when her attention was focused.

"You got any cinnamon rolls in there?" Andie motioned at the white pastry sack in Natalie's open briefcase. "I haven't had anything but coffee yet this morning and I'm starving," she added, hoping to draw her sister into a discussion on the importance of a good breakfast. Even though she was three years younger, Natalie could usually be counted on for a motherly lecture. "There was no time to fix anything before I left home."

Natalie plucked the bag out of her briefcase and tossed it at her sister. "They're low-fat bran muffins, but help yourself," she said, and stepped past Andie to peer more closely at the smeared writing. Andie opened the bag, trying to pretend the only thing on her mind at the moment was filling her stomach. She really was hungry; she hadn't lied about that. And if her mouth was full she couldn't answer the questions Natalie was going to start asking in about two minutes.

Natalie studied the wall intently, murmuring to herself as she tried to make out the words. "Be," she said, deciphering the first word easily enough. The next one was more difficult. "Fried...freed...freud... No, that doesn't make any sense." She glanced over at her sister for help, but Andie only shrugged and indicated that her mouth was full. "Butch." Natalie sighed and shook her head. "Why do bozos like this guy always think calling a woman a lesbian will make her run away and hide?"

Andie had to swallow before she could answer. "Maybe because that's what being called gay would do to them."

"Good point," Natalie said, and moved on to the next word.

Andie decided to try a little distraction. "How're Dad and the kids?" she asked. Andie's two youngest were spending the summer with their grandfather at Moose Lake in northern Minnesota. Her oldest, eighteen-year-old Kyle, was in Los Angeles with their father and stepmother number two—stepmother number one, the secretary he'd eloped with, hadn't lasted long. "Are they whining to come home yet?"

"Nope. Emily's in love with the boy who sells bait at the marina, and she's developed a passionate interest in fishing." Natalie flashed a quick, commiserating look at her sister. "Nothing to worry about. He's fifteen and doesn't even know she's alive."

"Thank God," Andie murmured. Emily was only twelve.

"Christopher is learning to windsurf. They said to say hi." Natalie settled her glasses more firmly on her nose and leaned closer to the wall. "Not butch," she mumbled. "Botch...beach..."

"And Dad?" Andie asked. "How's he doing?"

"The same as always, bless his pointed little head. He says the crime rate in Minneapolis has gone up since he retired from the force." A fond indulgent smile curved her lips. "He didn't actually say so but I'm sure he's convinced there's a direct correlation." Suddenly, her smile disappeared and her soft mouth thinned into a tight line. "It's bitch," she said flatly. With a grimace of distaste, she reached up and touched a fingertip to the words on the wall, following the faint outline of them beneath the blur of smeared red paint. "Be afraid, Bitch," she read, deciphering it at last. She turned a narrow-eyed stare on her sister. "I thought you said it was just the usual graffiti," she accused. "It sounds an awful lot like a threat to me."

"It *is* just the usual," Andie insisted.

"He's never threatened you before."

"And he hasn't threatened me now. I've been called a bitch before. And right to my face, I might add."

"By who?" Natalie demanded indignantly, aghast at the thought that anyone would call her sister a bitch. Andie was one of the sweetest, gentlest people she knew. And one of the loveliest. Even in her paint-stained overalls and heavy work boots, she looked like a delicate porcelain doll.

"By half the guys I beat out for this job, for starters. Some of my *brethren*—" she said the word with a faint underscoring of scorn "—are sure I was awarded the contract on this renovation strictly because of affirmative action. Or else they think I must be sleeping with everyone on the governing board of Belmont House. Male and female included, according to some of them." Andie shrugged, unconcerned by the slur on her reputation. "Either way, they're not shy about letting me know how they feel about it. I've told you that."

"I know, but..." Natalie shook her head in negation of what she, as a woman who also worked in a so-called man's field, knew all too well. "They act as if your work isn't good enough to speak for itself," she fumed, indignant on Andie's behalf. "You got this contract because you're one of the best up-and-coming contractors in the Twin Cities, with a great reputation for innovation and integrity. You always come in on budget and on time and no one has ever filed a complaint about you or the quality of your work. That should count for *something* with these knuckle-dragging Neanderthals."

"With some of these guys all that counts is the fact that I'm a woman. And speaking of Neanderthals..." Andie flashed a quick, sly grin that turned her from a pretty porcelain shepherdess into a cheeky gamine. "How's Lucas?"

Natalie rolled her eyes. "Oh, Lucas." She laughed softly, letting herself be drawn off the subject. Her husband's overdeveloped macho tendencies were a source of endless exasperation, and endless, albeit guilty, delight. The man was an ex-marine with a tattoo, an attitude and a king-size crush on his diminutive wife, even after nearly six years of marriage. "This weekend while we were up at the lake, he and Dad got together and tried to convince me that it was time to start cutting back on my hours and taking it easy."

"Already?" Andie surveyed her sister's trim figure. "You're not even showing yet."

"It's the cut of the jacket." Natalie smoothed a hand down the front of her brand-new apple green suit. "Believe me, I show plenty. I ended up wearing one of Lucas's shirts this weekend to hide the fact that I can't get my shorts buttoned anymore. Which, of course, only gave Dad more ammunition." She lowered her voice to a gruff rumble. "Any woman who is so obviously with child, little girl, has no damn business skulking around playing private eye, especially not when she's got a husband who's perfectly willing and able to support her. Not like your poor sister who—"

"Doesn't have a man to take care of her anymore," Andie finished in unison with her sister. She shook her head in amused disgust. "Now there's a man who deserves to be called a Neanderthal," she said, only half joking. "His attitudes are right out of the dark ages. If I've told him once, I've told him a thousand times that I have no intention of ever getting married again. Been there. Done that," she said, her tone implacable. "But does he listen? No-o-o, of course not. I'm just a woman. And a woman needs a man to look after her. I don't know how—"

"He worries about you," Natalie said, interrupting her rant. "We all do."

"There's no need," Andie quickly assured her. "I can take care of myself."

"You take care of everyone *but* yourself," her sister objected. "And you've been doing it ever since that slimeball you married took off for California with his bimbo secretary. Don't you think it's time to cut yourself some slack? The kids are well and happy and, thankfully, out of your hair for most of the summer. You've snagged a plum contract that will be a showcase for your company when it's finished. You're ahead of the game now, Andrea. You should take some time off just for yourself."

"And do what?" Andie asked, truly wanting to know. She'd almost forgotten what time off was for.

"Go to a movie or read a book or..." Natalie shrugged. "I don't know, take in an art gallery. Visit a museum. Get a pedicure. Or get really adventurous and find yourself a lover. God knows you're due." She reached out and touched her sister's cheek, tucking a wispy strand of silky blond hair behind Andie's ear in a familiar gesture of affection. "It's okay to ease up once in a while, honey."

"I can't afford to ease up," Andie said. "Not until after I finish this job."

"What do you mean, you can't *afford* to?" Natalie questioned, worry evident in her voice. "I thought business was good right now."

"It is."

"Then why can't you afford to take a few days off now and then?"

"Because my sterling reputation for integrity and innovation isn't the only reason I got the contract for Belmont House, that's why. I also underbid nearly every contractor in the Twin Cities to get it. And I stretched my resources to the limit to do it."

"Oh, Andrea. You're not going into the hole on this

one, are you? Not when you were so close to climbing out of it for good."

"Not if I finish Belmont House on time and on budget. And I will," Andie said fiercely.

"And you'll work yourself into the ground doing it, too."

"If I have to."

"Oh, Andrea," Natalie said again, obviously torn between pity, pride and admiration as she stared at her sister. Andrea might look like a china doll, but she was pure steel underneath, tempered and tested by time and circumstances. She'd been married at eighteen, two weeks out of high school, to a man who insisted her job was to stay home and take care of him and the family they hoped to have—despite the two academic scholarships she'd been offered. Thrilled to be living the dream of happily-ever-after with a seemingly devoted husband, she had gladly acceded to his wishes.

For eleven years Andrea had been a faithful, dutiful and loving wife. She'd done her husband's research and typed his papers so he could earn his M.B.A. She'd given wonderful little dinner parties to help him advance his career. She'd gone to the opera instead of movie musicals because that's what he liked. She'd dressed the way he wanted her to dress, thought the way he wanted her to think, and never, ever, overspent the weekly allowance he gave her. And then, when their third child was barely out of diapers, he'd left her and run off with his secretary. Almost overnight, Andrea lost nearly everything that mattered to her: her husband, her home, her standard of living, her standing in the community, her self-respect. Her identity. She lost everything except her children.

With no skills to speak of and support payments that barely stretched to the end of the month, Andrea had taken a long, hard look at what the world had to offer a woman in her circumstances and had decided that trade school was the answer.

Nine years later, the woman who had once defined herself by the lightness of her soufflés and the flawless finish of her husband's white shirts spent her days laying pipe, hammering up Sheetrock and wrestling with plumbing fixtures that weighed nearly as much as she did. With hard work, grit and the impetus of desperation, Andrea had made a new life for herself and her children. She'd put everything on the line, driving herself to exhaustion and beyond to get where she was.

Now it looked as if she was about to do it again.

Natalie wanted to tell her that she didn't have to work this hard, didn't have to put her future in jeopardy, that her family would be more than happy to help her. But she knew Andrea wouldn't listen. She would insist, as she had from the beginning, that she could handle it by herself.

"Is this job really important enough for you to risk everything you've worked for?" Natalie asked.

"You know it is," Andie said quietly. "With all the publicity it'll get when it's done, I'll be in a position to turn down jobs instead of pounding the pavement looking for them. I hope," she added, automatically reaching down to rap the walnut paneling in an effort to ward off bad luck.

"Well, then, it's even more important for you to do something about this—" Natalie gestured at the paint-smeared wall "—other than just cleaning it up so the rest of your crew won't see it. Until now it's just been a minor inconvenience. If you let it go on, the next time it could be something that will set you way behind schedule or bust a huge hole in your budget."

Andie had thought of that, too. Like any good contractor, she'd made allowances in her estimate for cost overruns and other foul-ups, but the fudge factor was very small and a big screwup could cost her more than she could afford in terms of time *or* money. But she didn't see any alternative. "What would you suggest I do?" she asked.

"You should report it to the police," Natalie said. "Let them get to work catching this guy for you."

"Oh, right," Andie scoffed. "And have Dad hear about it five minutes after the ink dries on the complaint? He'd be down here with a whole cadre of his police cronies, taking over, trying to protect me, treating me like the fragile little woman he thinks we both are. No, thanks." She stuck out her chin. "I can take care of this without his help. Or anyone else's."

"It's vandalism, Andrea. And trespassing. Breaking and entering, too, unless you're in the habit of leaving a job site unsecured."

"You know I'm not."

"Then whoever did this is guilty of more than one criminal act. Who knows what else he might do?"

"Whoever did this is guilty of sour grapes," Andie said. "He's angry about losing out to a woman and he wants me to know it. He wants to scare me, if he can, and send me running back to the kitchen, or wherever it is he thinks women belong. If I make a big fuss and call the police, then he's won, because he *wants* me to make a big fuss. It would just prove to him what he thinks he already knows—that women can't cut it. If I ignore him, then the fun's over and he'll pack up his can of spray paint and go home."

"And what if he doesn't?" Natalie pressed. "What if by ignoring him you just make him all the more determined to get a reaction? What if he decides to face you directly, so that you *can't* ignore him? Then what? Will you be able to handle *that* by yourself, too?"

"I won't have to. Guys who paint slogans on walls are like flashers. They get their jollies from the terrified reaction of their victims, and if the victim refuses to react, the game's over. It never escalates beyond that."

"Sometimes it does."

Andie shook her head. "No. This isn't like one of your cases, Natalie. The guy responsible for this isn't really a criminal."

"Yes," Natalie said firmly. "He is."

"Not in his own mind, he isn't. In his own mind, he's just striking a blow for the way he thinks things ought to be and never really were. Look, I know this guy, okay?" Andie reached out and put her hand on her sister's arm. "I know how he thinks because I've worked with him and men like him on dozens of construct—"

"Are you saying you *know* who's doing this? And you haven't reported him? Andrea, that's craz—"

"No. No, of course not. I didn't mean that I actually know who it is. I just..." She lifted her hands, splaying them in front of her chest as she tried to explain. "I meant that whoever did that—" she gestured toward the wall "—could be any one of a dozen guys I've worked with over the years. One of those guys who taped the centerfolds from *Hustler* where I'd be sure to see them, or the clown who put the vibrator in my tool belt or the foreman who arranged for me to get the hardest, dirtiest jobs he could find—jobs that were usually assigned to apprentices with way more experience than I had—and then stood around, waiting to gloat when I complained that it was too hard. But I didn't complain. And I didn't cry. I didn't respond in any way at all except to do my job as best I could. Pretty soon they stopped trying to get a rise out of me and let me get on with my job in peace. And that's what's going to happen here. If I refuse to respond, he'll give up and go away and that'll be the end of it."

Natalie could only stare at her. "I had no idea it had been that bad." She reached out, taking both of her sister's hands in hers. "Why didn't you tell me?"

"Because you would have sympathized and fussed over me. And you would have told Lucas, and he would have wanted to bust some heads. And Dad would have blustered and roared and tried to talk me into letting him support me and the kids. And I was so scared, I might have given in and let you all take care of me." Andie squeezed Natalie's fingers and let them go. "I needed to learn how to take care of myself."

"But at what cost?" Natalie said.

"Hey, it isn't all bad or I wouldn't still be in the business. The pay is much better than I could make working in an office. I've got union benefits. I'm my own boss. And I'm in better shape than I've ever been." She lifted her arm, flexing a slender biceps to illustrate her point and make her sister smile. "Besides, not every guy in construction is a jerk. Most of them are just normal working class stiffs, trying to make a living the best way they know how, same as me. Some of them even wish me well. This—" she rapped the paint-stained plaster with her knuckles "—is just some guy who hasn't learned yet that there's no such thing as a man's job or a woman's job. He thinks—"

The sound of a wolf whistle sliced through the air, floating in through the half-open front door. "Oh, baby...baby...look at those sweet cheeks!" called a female voice from outside.

Raucous feminine laughter followed the comment.

"You just ignore her, darlin', and come right on over here to Mama," yelled someone else. "I'll make you feel so-o-o good!"

Inside the Belmont House the two sisters looked at each other. "Were you expecting Lucas to meet you here?" Andie asked with a cheeky little grin.

2

THE WOMAN who'd offered the pithy, one-line commentary on the desirability of Jim Nicolosi's butt was of medium height and sturdy build, with streaks of iron gray in her short dark hair. She wore a tool belt around her waist. Jim tossed her an easy grin, not the least bit disconcerted to have his anatomy commented on so publicly.

"Why thank you, ma'am," he said, as he prepared to run the gauntlet of three women standing on the brick walkway in front of Belmont House, sharing coffee and conversation before they started their day's work. "It's always nice to know you're appreciated."

"Oh, I could appreciate you all right," said the woman who had referred to herself as Mama. She was all of about twenty-three years old, with a wild tangle of blond, corkscrew curls tumbling to her shoulders and the beautifully sculpted torso of a dedicated bodybuilder. "Give me thirty minutes and I could appreciate you into blissful exhaustion."

"*Tiffany!*" admonished the third woman in scandalized tones. She was the tallest of the three, with the pronounced features of an American Indian incongruously set off by a deep auburn braid and striking green eyes. "That's an outrageous thing to say to a stranger," she scolded softly, then demurely lowered her gaze when Jim turned to smile at her.

"But I *am* outrageous," Tiffany insisted with a throaty purr. "And you like outrageous women, don't you, sweet cheeks?" She gave Jim a come-hither glance that was hot enough to melt steel. "There's a gazebo out behind this old barn we could use if you're interested."

"Well, now...that's certainly an intriguing proposition." Jim let his gaze wander down the length of her truly magnificent body, giving her the same kind of once-over she'd given him. "But I've got this old war injury..." He let his voice trail off regretfully.

"I can work around it," she promised.

"Down, girl," said the older woman with a laugh. "You're scaring the poor man."

"He doesn't look scared to me." She lifted her gaze to Jim's face, fluttering her lashes seductively. "You scared of me, sweet cheeks?"

"You've got me shaking in my boots," Jim replied, the roguish gleam in his eyes belying his fainthearted words.

"I can start something else shaking if you—"

"Tiffany, let the poor man be, now," the older woman chided, a bit more sharply this time. "One of these days, I swear, girl, you're going to end up in the middle of a sexual-harassment suit." She looked over at Jim. "What can I do for you?"

"Ah...excuse me?" Jim was suddenly at a loss for words. The woman looked deadly serious all of a sudden. He could take teasing innuendo in his stride and toss it back without thinking twice, but a serious proposition from a woman who was probably old enough to be his mother was another matter entirely. He wasn't sure how to respond.

Tiffany snickered. "Talk about scaring the poor

man," she muttered, sotto voce. "He thinks you just made a pass at him."

The older woman shook her head in amused exasperation. "We've established that you're not here to pick up women, sweet cheeks, so what do you want? You an inspector? A supplier? Looking for a job? What?"

"Oh." Relief and embarrassment washed through Jim in equal measures. He'd thought...well, what they thought he'd been thinking. He only hoped he wasn't blushing. "I'm here about a job. I was told I'd need to talk to Andrea Wagner about it. Would that be you?" he asked, although he knew it wasn't. He'd been thoroughly briefed and he knew what Andrea Wagner looked like from the snapshot he'd been shown. But he was posing as a job applicant, and a job applicant wouldn't know unless he asked.

"I wish," the woman said. "I'm Dot Lancing, one of the carpenters on this job. This is Mary Free." She indicated the tall American Indian woman. "She's our electrician. And the man-eater is Tiffany Wilkes, electrician's apprentice. The antisocial type, sitting on the steps there and pretending he doesn't know us—" she jerked her thumb backward, toward the house, and Jim followed it with his gaze, noticing the man for the first time "—is Pete Lindstrom, carpenter. Say hello, Pete."

Pete bobbed his head once, giving a grunt that might have been "hello," and went back to his coffee and newspaper.

Jim nodded in return, acknowledging the introduction in the same manner, then turned back to Dot. "And Andrea Wagner?"

"Andie's in the house." She pointed toward the wide front door. "Right through there."

"Thanks." Jim touched his finger to his forehead in a brief salute and started up the front steps and across the porch toward the half-open door, keeping to one side to avoid disturbing Pete Lindstrom again.

"Oh. And sweet cheeks?" Dot waited until Jim turned around to look back at her. "Don't try to charm her. You'll end up out here on that cute little fanny of yours if you do."

Jim nodded and turned back toward the front door. He'd heard Andrea Wagner was a hard case who didn't take crap from anybody, least of all a man. He'd thought at the time that it was a shame such a pretty woman was a ball-buster. He thought it even more of a shame when he stepped through the door of Belmont House and saw her standing there in the soaring, two-story foyer.

Actually, for a moment he thought he was looking at a mirror image, or twins. Two women stood facing each other, shoulders hunched slightly, heads together like schoolgirls sharing secrets. They were nearly the same height, with the same pale, wheat-colored blond hair and delicate build. But the differences between them quickly became apparent.

One wore her hair in a sleek, chic businesswoman style that swung enticingly around her sculpted jawline. Her suit was equally sleek and streamlined, skimming a trim figure and making the most of a great pair of legs. She wore shiny gold hoops in her ears, a gold lapel pin shaped like a crescent moon on the left shoulder of her suit, and soft red lipstick on her generous mouth. Much of her apparent height, he realized, was achieved by a pair of killer high heels. In her bare feet she probably wouldn't top out at more than five foot two.

The other woman was taller by at least three inches. Her pale blond hair was as short as a boy's. She was dressed like a boy, too, in a sleeveless ribbed T-shirt—the kind old men and bodybuilders wore—under paint-splattered denim overalls. A tool belt rode her slender hips. Heavy work boots were laced tight to her ankles. Her face was bare of makeup. And yet, somehow, she looked just as feminine, even more feminine, perhaps, than the woman standing next to her in green high heels and a matching power suit.

The extreme shortness of her hair exposed the delicate curve of her ears and seemed to emphasize the fragility of her jaw and the slenderness of her neck. The lack of lipstick on her mouth only served to draw more attention to the sculpted shape and soft pink color of her lips. Even the rough masculinity of her clothes conspired against her, making her seem even more intensely female in contrast.

"Ah...excuse me, ladies," Jim said, and discovered another major difference between the two women when they turned their heads to look at him.

The sleek one had big brown eyes, as dark as chocolate and brimming with curiosity and intelligence, like those of an eager, bright-eyed terrier. The other one had eyes the color of a Minnesota sky on a bright winter's day—a pale, piercing blue, as pure and clear as mountain ice, and he couldn't read the look in them.

The two women examined him for a moment as he stood there in the doorway, their eyes dancing with some secret merriment, and then they looked back at each other. "Not Lucas," the one in the green suit said, and they both burst into giggles.

Jim shifted awkwardly, resisting the urge to check his

fly, and wondered if it was just his day to be made uncomfortable by women. It wasn't a feeling he liked, and normally he wouldn't have stood for it without getting back some of his own. But he had a job to do.

"Is one of you Andrea Wagner?" he said, looking back and forth between them as if he didn't know who was who.

"I'm Andrea Wagner," Andie said, without moving from where she was. "And this is my sister, Natalie Bishop-Sinclair." Another giggle escaped when they caught each other's eyes. "Natalie was just leaving. Weren't you, Nat?" she said.

"Yes. I'm leaving. Definitely." She moved to her briefcase, closed it, then picked it up. "Promise me you'll at least think about what I said," she ordered softly as she paused to press her cheek to her sister's.

Andie returned the caress. "I promise I'll *think* about it," she murmured, her tone of voice saying that was all she would do.

"God, you're stubborn," Natalie lamented. She turned slightly toward the door, where Jim stood waiting, then turned back to her sister with an impish grin. "If you won't take my advice about the graffiti artist, you should at least consider taking my advice about that other little matter we talked about."

"Other matter?"

"You're due, honey." Natalie tilted her head toward the man standing just inside the door, and waggled her eyebrows. "If you get my drift."

Andie got it.

"Goodbye, Natalie," she said, giving her sister a little push toward the door to reinforce the message.

With a low laugh and one last appreciative glance at

the man, who politely moved to one side to let her pass, Natalie went.

Andie turned to her unexpected guest. "I'm sorry about that," she apologized, hoping her cheeks weren't as red as they felt. She could just murder her sister sometimes! "We weren't laughing at you. It was just a—" she fluttered one hand "—sister thing that kind of got out of hand for a minute there."

"No problem. I've got three sisters of my own. I know how you girls get," Jim said, then wondered if he should have said "women" instead.

You never knew with these high-octane feminist types. Most of them tended to get pretty irate when their dignity was offended. And from what he'd been told, Andrea Wagner was as likely to hand him his head on a platter as look at him if he put her back up. And damn if she didn't look kind of red faced already, and he'd barely even opened his mouth. But she simply nodded, apparently unoffended by his slip of the tongue. Or at least not offended enough to comment on it.

He held out his hand. "Jim Nicolosi," he said, noting her almost infinitesimal hesitation before she reached out with her own and accepted it. He filed that tidbit of information away while also noting that her hand was small, delicate and callused. The handshake was firm but brief.

"What can I do for you?" she asked, and there was nothing playful or giggly about her now. She was all-business.

Remembering Dot Lancing's warning about trying to charm her, Jim decided he'd better be likewise. "Dave Carlisle sent me over. He said you were looking for a carpenter. Someone who was good at finish work. I'm here for the job."

"So Dave sent you, did he?" Andrea said, her lips pursed in thought as she considered what he'd said. "Hmm."

Dave Carlisle was one of the good guys in the business. He didn't discriminate, not against women or minorities. Getting the job done and getting it done right was all that mattered to him. He'd sent her lots of people during the years she'd been in business for herself, knowing she'd teach apprentices right and treat them fairly, male or female. When Dave sent them to her, she usually took them on if she could, knowing he wouldn't send her anyone who wasn't qualified.

This guy didn't look like an apprentice, though. He was too old, for one thing. Most apprentices were closer to Tiffany's age. Still, he could be someone looking to make a midlife career change. Although he probably wasn't quite old enough to qualify as someone who had actually *reached* the midpoint of his life yet. Or he could have gotten a late start, as she had, which would explain why he was still an apprentice in his...oh, early to mid-thirties, she decided. Which was probably why Dave had sent him to her. Dave knew she was always willing to give someone with a hard-luck story a break.

Not that she was interested in this guy's story. She just wanted a finish carpenter to replace the one who had bailed out on her last week.

But did she want one badly enough to risk the harmony of her crew?

Jim Nicolosi was a wickedly handsome man, way too handsome for his own—or anyone else's—good. A walking invitation to sex and sin, he was at least six feet tall, with broad, heavily muscled shoulders, narrow hips and long legs encased in faded denim. His hair was dark brown without a hint of red, and he wore it longer than she wore hers; it curled temptingly over his ears and touched the collar of his shirt in back. His eyes were brown, too, and there was something about the roguish gleam in them that told her he knew exactly how good-looking he was, and what effect those good looks had on the opposite sex. Of course, he'd be a fool if he didn't know, but that was beside the point. He'd be a major distraction on the job, no doubt about it and...

And Andie realized she was guilty of sexist thinking and told herself to stop it. Jim Nicolosi's looks had nothing to do with whether or not he was qualified for the job. And other people's—okay, *women's*—reaction to his looks was their problem, not his. She had to be scrupulously fair about this, especially because she wasn't unaffected by his looks herself.

Her sister's voice echoed in her memory. *God knows you're due.*

Andie had to admit in her heart of hearts that, by any standard known to modern woman, Natalie was right. She *was* due! It had been... Lord, she couldn't remember when the last time had been. Years ago. Literally. And this man was enough to make a nun start thinking about things she was better off ignoring.

"You do know this is just an apprentice's job, don't you?" Andie asked, hoping for an easy out. "With an apprentice's pay. It's not a journeyman's position."

"Yes, I know. Dave was clear on that. But I haven't got my journeyman's certification yet, so it's okay. I had an accident a while ago that cost me a lot of time and sort of screwed things up for me."

It was close enough to the truth, Jim told himself. Hell, it *was* the truth, as far as it went. He had had an accident and he didn't have a journeyman's certification. The reasons didn't matter, especially when the bare facts worked so well. He'd been told she was a sucker for a hard-luck story.

He could see it was true. The sudden compassion in her expression was as clear as the color of her eyes. She was going to offer him the job. He could feel it.

"This accident of yours..." she began, steeling herself to ask the questions she knew she must. He didn't look disabled, but you could never tell, and she couldn't afford to hire someone who wasn't going to be able to stick it out to the end, no matter who had recommended him, "...it didn't leave you with any kind of disability that would make you unable to do the job, did it?"

"I can do the job," he said sharply, stung by the dispassionate way she'd asked the question. And the fact that he'd been wrong. He'd been so sure the next words out of her mouth would be a job offer, and then she'd opened her soft pink lips to coolly question his competence. He was just a little bit sensitive about that—okay, a lot sensitive—and, however unknowingly, she'd made a direct hit on his ego by questioning his ability.

He'd started to tell her where she could get off when he saw something in her eyes, some flicker that presaged a refusal, and he quickly changed tactics. He couldn't do what he'd been hired to do if he didn't get hired for this job first. And aggravating her was not the way to get himself hired.

"I have a little bit of a problem with heights," he admitted reluctantly, casting a wary glance at the scaffolding against the far wall. Women were suckers for vulnerability in a man, or so his sisters were always saying. "I'm not real comfortable going up on roofs, for instance. I fell from one." Again, it was true as far as it went; it just didn't go all the way. "But I can do everything else," he added quickly, in case he'd taken the vulnerability thing a bit too far. "All the way from basic framing to custom cabinetry, hardwood floors, fancy trim, whatever you want done. I've had some experience with tile work, too. And I'm pretty good at turning out decorative spindles for something like that," he said, gesturing toward the grand staircase, which was missing several of its balusters.

Andie nodded, impressed and tempted in spite of herself. She could really use someone with his talents. Especially someone who came at an apprentice's salary. Still she hesitated, looking for a way out. This man meant trouble for her, one way or another. She just knew it.

"My crew is mostly women," she told him, still trying to find something to make *him* decide against the job. "The sprinkler fitter finished up last week, so I don't have many men working for me right now. My mason, Dan Johnston, is only here intermittently, between other jobs, so you won't be able to count on him or his crew to buddy around with. In fact, I have only three full-time guys on my payroll right now—Pete Lindstrom, who's a journeyman carpenter, and two apprentices, Booker Pitt and Matthew Barnes. Both of them are just kids, really, working construction during summer vacation. And I'll tell you right now, the apprentices do most of the grunt work around here, just like on any other job."

"Of course," Jim agreed, refusing to be put off.

"And just because I'm a woman doesn't mean I'll be any easier on you than a man would be. I expect my employees to be here on time and put in a full day's work for a full day's pay," she said, in case he had any misconceptions. "I won't tolerate loafing on the job."

"Of course not," Jim agreed again.

"I also expect the apprentices to jump when a journeyman says jump. And most of my journeymen are women." Andie peered up at him, giving him a narrow-eyed stare from beneath sweeping lashes. "I don't want you around if you're going to have problems taking orders from a woman."

"Like I said, I have three sisters, all older than me. I'm used to being ordered around by women."

The grin he gave her was sweet and disarming, with none of the sexual overtones of the one he'd flashed at the women outside. *I'm just a big, old, harmless, brotherly lug,* it seemed to say. At least, he hoped that's what it said.

He wasn't feeling very brotherly at the moment, not when she stood there staring up at him with those big blues eyes of hers fixed so earnestly on his face, her full pink lips pursed in concentration, and a cute little frown knitting her arched brows. She had the clearest, palest skin he'd ever seen, as fine and translucent as his two-year-old niece's, and her short, wispy hair looked like silk. She was close enough now that he could see the faint line of a tiny, intriguing scar just beneath the curve of her lower lip, as well as the baby-size pearl studs she wore in the delicate lobes of her ears. He could smell her perfume, too.

He hadn't expected a woman like her—an avowed feminist, a reputed ball-buster, a construction worker, for God's sake!—to be wearing pearl earrings. Or perfume, either. But there it was.

The scent was light and clean smelling, kind of fresh and delicate, like the woman who wore it. And something about it reminded him of the first time he'd ever had sex. Charlie—that was it, he decided. Patty Newcomb had been wearing Charlie cologne when she'd finally surrendered to him in the back seat of his dad's Chevy Impala during the Saturday Night Monster Movie Extravaganza at the Skyline Drive-In. Ever since then, that particular scent had always made him as horny as a hound dog.

And that wouldn't do at all.

Sex would only get in the way of what he had to do.

"As long as nobody asks me to make coffee, we'll all get along fine," he said, trying for a little humor to lighten the sudden intensity of his feelings.

She didn't seem to realize he'd made a joke. "All right," she said with a sigh. "The first two weeks, you're on probation, just like everybody else. If you're still here after that, consider yourself hired."

LATER THAT NIGHT Jim called the number he'd been given and filed his first report. "I got the job," he said to the man who answered the phone. "I start tomorrow morning."

Jim listened for a moment, then said reasuringly, "No, she doesn't suspect a thing."

3

DOT LANCING POKED HER HEAD into what was being turned into the new basement powder room adjacent to what would eventually be the offices of Belmont House. "I'm taking off," she said, speaking to the pair of denim-sheathed legs sticking out from under the vanity. "Andie?" She rapped on the custom marble countertop.

Andie jumped, but managed not to squeal. "What?"

"Time to call it a day, kiddo."

"Already?" Andie stopped wrestling with the stubborn coupling and turned her wrist to squint at her watch, careful not to whack herself in the head with the long-handled pipe wrench she was using to give herself more leverage. It was nearly six o'clock. How had it gotten to be so late so soon? "Hold up a minute, would you?" she said, reaching down to set the pipe wrench on the floor by her thigh.

Dot leaned a shoulder against the doorjamb. "What's up?" she asked, as Andie squirmed out from under the sink and sat up.

"What do you think of the new guy?"

"Who? Sweet cheeks?"

Andie frowned. "I wish you wouldn't call him that."

"Merely stating the obvious."

"Obvious or not, it's unprofessional," Andie chided

her. "Sexual harassment works both ways, you know. He could file a complaint with the union."

Dot shrugged. "I don't think you have to worry about that. It's all good clean fun, and he gives as good as he gets."

Andie knew he did; she'd heard him trading risqué innuendos with Tiffany all afternoon. She'd even heard shy Mary Free laugh once at some sally he'd made. But that still didn't make it right. "It's highly unprofessional."

"All right." Dot didn't need to be told twice. "I'll pass the word."

"I'd appreciate it." Andie pushed herself to her feet and stood. "So—" she clasped her hands behind her back and raised them as high as she could, stretching taut muscles "—how did he do today?"

"I started him off easy, putting a second coat of Spackle on the walls in the upstairs sitting room. When he finished that, I put him to work on the marble mantelpiece in the master bedroom," she said, giving her boss a conspiratorial grin. Restoring marble, especially elaborately carved marble, was a tedious, exacting job. It was also one that required a certain degree of finesse. "He knows what he's doing and he's got a real feel for the work, so I left him to it," Dot said, and coming from her it was high praise. "Hard to believe he's only an apprentice."

"Apparently, he had some sort of accident," Andie said. "It put him behind a bit, I guess."

"So that's it," Dot murmured. "I wondered about the scars."

"Scars?"

"He yanked his T-shirt up a couple of times to wipe

his face while he was working on the mantel. He's got a couple of pretty gruesome-looking scars on the lower right side of his back. You can just barely see them above those sweet ch...above the waistband of his jeans."

"Did he say what happened?"

"I didn't ask him," Dot said. "Tiffany started to, but he cut her off real quick with some joke about an old war injury. I figured he probably didn't want to talk about it." She pushed herself away from the doorjamb. "A few of us are meeting over at Varga's for a drink to celebrate Tiffany's pregnancy test not turning pink. You wanna come?"

"No, thanks." Andie shook her head. "I want to finish this," she said, gesturing at the sink.

"It'll still be here tomorrow."

"Not if I finish it tonight, it won't be," Andie said. She was already back down on the floor, twisting around so she could slide under the sink.

"Don't stay here too late by yourself, okay?" Dot said.

Andie paused, her hands on the edge of the vanity in preparation for dragging herself under, and looked up, alerted by something in Dot's tone of voice.

"I read what was on the foyer wall before I patched it," Dot said.

"Then you should know it's nothing to be concerned about. Just some jerk venting his spleen against women construction workers."

"Probably," Dot agreed, but she didn't sound entirely convinced. "Don't stay here too late by yourself, anyway, just in case. Lock up and leave before it gets dark."

"Yes, Mother," Andie said. "Give Tiffany my congratulations on not being pregnant. And don't let her have more than one Screaming Orgasm or she'll be in the same fix next month." With that, Andie propelled herself back under the sink, ending the discussion.

IT WAS AFTER SEVEN when Andie finally got the sink installed to her satisfaction. The tiny basement powder room was more modern and utilitarian than the three period bathrooms being so meticulously restored in the rooms upstairs, but that didn't mean she was going to rush the job or be any less exacting in her work. If a job was worth doing, it was worth doing well, whether that job be making a soufflé or installing a lavatory sink.

She plucked a soft rag out of the back pocket of her overalls and wiped the fine layer of powdery drywall dust off of the marble countertop, pleased with the way the pale rose of the porcelain drop-in sink looked against the creamy, pink-veined marble. Tomorrow the tile could be installed, and after that, the delicate rosebud wallpaper. When the reproduction Queen Anne vanity mirror arrived and was finally hung over the sink, the tiny, perfect powder room would be complete. Ahead of schedule.

With a satisfied smile, Andie shut off the light and made her way through the dim, half-finished basement offices toward the light shining in through the open door at the top of the stairs. It was natural light that greeted her—during midsummer in Minnesota, it didn't even begin to get dark until after nine o'clock—so instead of locking up and heading out to her truck, she made a slow survey of the empty rooms, checking progress, making mental notes to herself about what had been accomplished that day and what still needed doing. Assuring herself that everything was as it should be.

Belmont House was a Queen Anne Victorian, circa 1895, with a steep, hipped roof, shaped, parapeted gables and patterned masonry walls. A deep porch supported by classic columns and decorated with cornice-line dentils extended across the front and around both sides of the house, accentuating the deliberate asymmetry of the facade. Large bay windows, a partially cantilevered second story and a tower at the left front corner added to the stately charm of the house. It had been built by a wealthy industrialist who had made his fortune in iron ore and shipping in Duluth, Minnesota. His bride had found the winters too harsh and cold, there on the banks of Lake Superior, however, so he had built her this imposing Victorian castle overlooking the Lake of the Isles in Minneapolis.

Unfortunately, forty years of a reportedly happy marriage had left the couple childless, and the house had been taken over by a cousin upon the death of the industrialist's widow, who willed it to a nephew, who had neither the wherewithal nor the inclination to maintain the huge old place. Eventually, it had passed into the hands of the city in lieu of unpaid taxes, and in due course had been purchased for the proverbial song by an historical foundation that was now turning it into a piece of living history. When the renovation was complete and the decorator had furnished the restored rooms with period antiques and fine reproductions, the lovely old mansion would be open for tours, for private parties and charity events.

Even now, Andie had only to close her eyes to see the

partially restored estate as it had been and would be again. At the moment, however, the floors were still several steps away from the final refinishing; the walls were unpainted—and nonexistent in some cases—with bare studs and wiring exposed. The grand staircase was grand only in scale; the marble fireplace was stained with years of neglect; the windows were grimy with dust and the grit of ongoing construction. A crystal chandelier, an exact reproduction of the original, sat in an open wooden crate on the floor in the dining room, with packing material strewn over the hardwood floor around it like tissue paper around the tree on Christmas morning. Light from the low-slanting sun found the faceted crystal prisms and sent colorful squares of light dancing across the floor, silent promise of how it would look when the house was restored to its former glory.

Andie smiled at her own fanciful thoughts and followed the pattern of light toward the crate, like Gretel following a trail of bread crumbs through the forest. She crouched down and carefully, using the strength of her legs and simple leverage, maneuvered the wooden lid of the crate back into place. Although the chandelier was a reproduction and not a Victorian antique like many of the other fixtures that would grace the finished house, it was still deserving of special care. Tomorrow she would remind her crew about leaving such a fragile item exposed to drywall dust and possible accidents.

That task taken care of, she headed upstairs to where most of the day's work had been done to see what had been accomplished. The third floor, with its servants' bedrooms and the unused nursery wing, was almost complete. The walls had been drywalled and spackled and, in some cases, primed and ready for the first coat of paint. The simple pierced cornices had been restored and reinstalled. The modest lighting fixtures had been rewired and brought up to code. Booker, the apprentice plumber, appeared to be making excellent progress in the spartan servants' bathroom with its unadorned bathtub and pedestal sink, classic high-water-tank toilet and plain white brick walls. Andie was more than pleased with the quality of his work.

Progress on the second floor was advancing at a slower pace due to the increased complexity of the job. Walls and ceilings were decorated with carved wainscoting, intricate plaster panels and elaborate cornices and baseboards. The bathrooms—two of them—were marvels of late Victorian technology and ostentatiousness, with painted porcelain fixtures, rolltop tubs encased in mahogany surrounds and marble tile, all of which had to be carefully and laboriously restored, or replaced if restoration proved impossible.

Dot and her busy crew of apprentices had made impressive inroads on the wainscoting in the wide center hall. Mary Free and Tiffany had finished with the wiring in all but two of the five bedrooms, cleverly concealing the evidence of their work behind baseboards and chair rails. And Jim Nicolosi had left the walls in the upstairs sitting room smooth and even, ready for sanding and, eventually, the application of the hand-printed yellow silk moiré wallpaper the designer had selected for the room.

Of course, anybody with a little experience could spackle a wall, Andie told herself as she headed toward the open door of the master bedroom to see if her newest employee was really as good as Dot said he was. The real test would be the mantelpiece.

He was definitely as good as Dot said.

Andie put her hand out, running her fingertips lightly over the section of jade green marble he had so thoroughly and delicately cleaned, a few square inches at a time, using cotton pads, Q-tips and marble-stain remover. A few chipped places had been carefully filled in with colored marble glue, which, when completely dry, would be rubbed down with fine wet-and-dry sandpaper until it blended in. The work was meticulous, as painstakingly executed as if she had done it herself. It seemed Jim Nicolosi was a man who knew the virtue of patience when it came to doing a job right. A man with...

Andie felt a fizzle of heat work its way up her spine as a comment Tiffany had made that afternoon suddenly came back to her. She hadn't heard Jim's response, but it had brought a low, throaty laugh from Tiffany and an appreciative chuckle from Dot.

"You've got slow hands, sweet cheeks," Tiffany had purred. "I like a man with slow hands."

Andie passing by the open door on her way downstairs to the basement at the time, hadn't given it another thought.

Until now.

Now it brought quick color to her cheeks and filled her mind with all sorts of erotic images. Images of what it would be like to be touched by a man with slow hands.

"Darn you, Natalie," she muttered, as the fizzle of heat burst and blossomed outward like a firecracker, setting her breasts and stomach and thighs to tingling with seductive warmth.

If Natalie hadn't made that idiotic comment about being duc for a lover, Andie wouldn't be standing in front of the mantel now, fingertips pressing against the cool green marble, staring at Jim Nicolosi's exquisite handiwork and wondering what it would feel like to have him touch her in the same careful, painstaking way.

Or in any way at all.

She knew *exactly* how long it had been since she'd been touched by a man. Eight years. It had been eight long years since the disastrous one-night stand she'd had with her ex-husband's ex-business partner. He'd been solicitous and understanding. She'd been desperate to prove she was still a desirable woman; desperate, too, for revenge against her cheating husband. And who better for both purposes than a man she knew would go running to Kevin with the news the minute he left her bed? The experience was ultimately unsatisfying, in more than just the physical. He hadn't desired her as a unique, individual woman, any more than she'd desired him as an individual man.

Revenge was less than sweet when the object of that revenge was twelve hundred miles away with a new wife.

Andie hadn't really been tempted since. But she was tempted now. *God knows you're due.*

"Yeah, right," Andie muttered to herself. "As if it were up to me."

Jim Nicolosi hadn't so much as cast a speculative glance in her direction, and he wouldn't. Not with sexy, saucy Tiffany Wilkes ready, willing and oh-so-available. Next to the twenty-three-year-old electrician's apprentice, Andie looked like a boy. A man with a rogue's gleam in his eyes like Jim Nicolosi, wouldn't be interested in a boy. Besides, she was older than he was, she had three kids, and she might be due for sex, but she certainly wasn't crazy. Only a crazy woman would get involved with an employee.

Besides, she wasn't looking for a relationship.

She didn't have time for a relationship.

She didn't *want* a relationship.

Not now.

Not ever.

Case closed, as Natalie would say. *End of story.*

Andie pushed herself away from the mantel, turned around and ran smack-dab into a hard male chest. She let out a startled shriek and threw up her hands, ready to defend herself even as she stumbled backward.

"Hey, there, boss lady," Jim said, grabbing her by the upper arms to keep her from crashing into the mantel. "Take it easy."

"Take it easy?" Andie clutched the front of his T-shirt in both hands. "Take it easy! How am I supposed to take it easy when people keep sneaking up on me?"

"I'm sorry. I didn't mean to—"

"Natalie tiptoed in this morning and almost scared me to death. A minute ago Dot banged on the counter and I nearly whacked my head on the pipes."

"I'm sorry," he said again, "I—"

"And now you come creeping up behind me like... like..." She clamped her teeth together, appalled at the shrill sound of her own voice—and the way she stood there, clutching the front of his T-shirt as if she were a frightened child.

Darn Natalie! And darn Dot, too, while she was at it. They had her jumping at shadows, thinking the weasel who was drawing on her walls had decided to take a more direct approach, when deep inside she knew better. She felt like such a fool! And probably looked like one, too, from the perspective of the man whose T-shirt she was mangling in her fists.

She uncurled her fingers, patting the rumpled fabric of Jim Nicolosi's T-shirt as if she could smooth it. "Sorry," she said sheepishly, without looking at him.

"I'm the one who's sorry." He rubbed his hands lightly up and down her arms in a reflex effort to comfort her. "I should have called your name or whistled or something."

"Yes," she said, trying to sound forceful instead of frightened, but sounding almost sulky instead. "You should have."

"Next time I will."

"See that you—" she lifted her gaze to his to give her words more power "—do," she finished weakly, as all thoughts of Natalie and Dot and the hypothetically violent tendencies of the graffiti terrorist vanished from her mind.

Close up, Jim Nicolosi's eyes weren't really brown. Not completely. They were flecked with bits of amber and gold, catching and reflecting the light like fifty-year-old brandy in a Waterford crystal. They were as hot as good brandy, too, and deceptively smooth, with enough kick to knock a woman flat on her back. Andie could almost feel herself falling.

"It isn't really as bad as all that, is it?"

"Huh?" she said stupidly, disconcerted by his eyes and the feel of his hands—his *slow* hands—on her bare arms; disconcerted by her own fevered imaginings of what those hands would feel like on the rest of her body.

"The mantel," Jim said. "I know I'm only an apprentice, but it can't be as bad as that." He cocked an eyebrow at her. "Can it?"

"Oh. Oh, the mantel. No, it's fine. Fine. It's just...ah, just..."

His mouth was beautifully formed. His lips were full, but not too full, with sharply defined edges and a pronounced dip in the center. It was a sensual mouth, a mouth made for long, slow kisses and whispering secrets in the dark.

"Just...?" he prompted, and a corner of his beautiful mouth lifted in a little half smile as he waited for her answer.

She was staring at him as if she'd never seen a man before. Her big blue eyes were as wide as saucers, their expression soft and unfocused and fathomless, as wondering and innocent as a baby's. Her soft pink lips were parted slightly, as if in invitation. Her pale, translucent cheeks were flushed with delicate color. And he could see her heart pounding like a dream in the little hollow at the base of her throat, as tempting as an exotic flower to a hungry bee.

Jim abruptly decided that sex wouldn't be all that much of a complication, after all, and he bent his head, seduced by the rapt look of fascination on her face, intent on accepting the invitation she had unwittingly offered.

For just a second, a mere moment in time, Andie acquiesced. Her chin lifted. Her eyelids fluttered. Her breath caught in her throat. She could feel the heat in him, the anticipation, the pure sexual speculation that was the overture to every first kiss. She could feel all those things in herself, reaching out, answering him.

Then suddenly, just before his lips touched hers, her

brain reconnected to reality. She gasped and pulled back. "What do you think you're doing?" she demanded, more of herself than of him.

He raised one eyebrow. "Kissing you?"

"No." She shrugged out from under his hands and stepped around him, away from temptation. "No, that's..."

He turned, pivoting to keep her in sight as she went around him.

"No," she said again. "That isn't what I meant," she lied, trying to find her way through the morass of tangled feelings—attraction, fascination, desire, fear—that seemed to be assaulting her from all sides. "I meant, what are you doing *here? Now?*"

"I work here, remember?" he said, sorting out her meaning easily enough. "I started this morning."

"It's way past quitting time. Everybody else left—" she glanced at her watch "—over an hour ago."

"You're still here," he pointed out.

"I'm the boss. I have a vested interest in working late."

"And I'm the newest employee. On probation," he reminded her. "I have a vested interest in working late, too, wouldn't you say?"

"I'm not impressed by brownnosers," she snapped, and was instantly contrite, even before she saw the way his eyebrows pulled together in a frown. "I'm sorry. That was rude and uncalled for, and I didn't mean it. I mean, I'm *not* impressed by brownnosers, but I didn't mean to imply that you...that..." She put one hand to her forehead, covering her eyes for a minute, and blew out a deep breath. "I'm sorry," she said simply, looking up at him with a rueful little smile. "I'm a little frazzled."

"You're upset."

"Yes. No." She took another deep breath and blew it out. "A little, I guess," she admitted.

"Why?" he asked, wondering if she'd tell him the truth.

She didn't. At least, not all of it. Not the real reason. "I had a granola bar for breakfast and a hard-boiled egg for lunch, and it's way past my dinnertime. I always get a little testy when I'm hungry. You can ask my kids," she added, throwing that little tidbit of information in just in case he was inclined to scramble her brains some more by trying to kiss her again. There was nothing like knowing a woman had kids to stop a man dead in his tracks. "They'll tell you."

"You've got kids?"

"Three." She held up the appropriate number of fingers. "The oldest one is eighteen."

"Eighteen?" He'd known she had kids, of course. He'd been briefed with all the pertinent facts, or so he'd thought. "You've got a kid who's eighteen years old?"

"He'll be going to UCLA this fall."

"You must have been a baby when you had him."

"I was twenty."

"Twenty," he repeated, and she watched him add it up. "You don't look thirty-eight. Hell, you barely look old enough to vote."

"Well." She shrugged, staunchly ignoring the flattery and the little spurt of pleasure it gave her. What was important was that he had all the necessary facts now; he wouldn't be coming on to her again, so she said, "You know what they say about looks being deceiving and all that."

"Yeah, I know what they say," he agreed, reading her easily enough. "Since you haven't eaten and I haven't eaten, whaddya say we go grab a bite somewhere?" he said, and then watched her eye's widen in surprise. It almost made him grin. She'd been so sure he'd back off, and so unprepared when he didn't. "We both have to eat," he added, before she could say no. "We might as well do it together...unless your kids are waiting for you...or you've got a date?"

"No, I—"

"Well, then, there's no problem, is there?"

"I'm filthy," she said, seizing on the first thing she could think of. It wouldn't have mattered if they were headed for a drink at Varga's; the place was a blue-collar juke joint. But dinner was another story. Any establishment where she'd actually want to eat probably wouldn't be thrilled to see a couple of paint-spattered, dust-covered construction workers walk in. "We're both filthy."

"That's okay. I know this great little hamburger joint out on Excelsior where the management isn't fussy about what you wear. It's in Glen Lakes, just before you get to Minnetonka. You probably pass right by it on your way home. The Golden Nugget?"

Andie shook her head. "I don't think—"

"Just a friendly meal," he hastened to assure her. "Two colleagues breaking bread together at the end of the day. I'll even promise not to suck up to the boss." He raised his hand and crossed his heart. "Scout's honor."

It was the reference to sucking up that got her. She already felt bad about calling him a brownnoser. "All right. But it's just a friendly business dinner, right? Nothing else."

"Strictly business," he agreed solemnly. "We'll talk about drywalling techniques and you can critique my first day on the job."

Andie laughed, suddenly looking forward to the evening ahead.

4

THE GOLDEN NUGGET was a tiny place in a small strip mall; it had a bar, a few large wooden booths along one wall and a few more Formica-topped tables scattered around. The chairs were chrome with imitation-leather seats, the napkins were paper and the decor was strictly accidental, consisting of various flyers advertising charity drives, lost pets and neighborhood softball games. Customers' business cards were tacked up on small bulletin boards around the room. Several framed magazine articles and newspaper columns clustered together on one wall declared that the restaurant served the best hamburgers in the Twin Cities. The smells wafting out of the kitchen reinforced that lofty assertion and made Andie's mouth water.

They settled across from each other in one of the empty booths and gave their order—two burgers, medium rare, and an order of onion rings—to the waiter. "So," Jim said. "How'd a nice girl like you end up wearing a tool belt and a hard hat?"

Andie gave him a cool look over the rim of her beer mug.

"Woman," he said, with an engaging little grin that apologized without admitting guilt. "I meant woman. How'd a nice woman like you end up in the construction business?"

"Why?" She put the heavy mug down, placing it

carefully, precisely, on the small, square paper napkin in front of her. "Is there something wrong with a woman being in the construction business?"

"No, of course not. It's just that it's a little unusual, is all. Until yesterday, I don't think I've ever seen more than one or two women on a job site at one time before."

"Get used to it," she advised dryly. "More and more women are entering trade school all the time."

"I don't see why they'd want to. It's hard, dirty work."

"No harder than waiting tables for a living. Or standing behind some department-store cosmetics counter, pushing lipstick and eyeliner for eight hours a day at minimum wage." Both of which Andie had done before she'd decided trade school was the answer to her problems. "The pay's a lot better in the trades. A *lot*," she emphasized. "The only way I could make more money without a college degree would be to shake my booty at someplace like the Gentleman's Lair." She shrugged, eyes downcast, her mouth turning up in a moue of self-deprecation as she ran her finger around the edge of her glass. "And I haven't got quite enough booty for that."

"Oh, I don't know." He turned his smile into an appreciative leer with the quirk of an eyebrow. "I'd pay to see you shake it."

She shot him a mildly censuring look from beneath her lashes. "This is supposed to be a friendly little dinner, remember? Let's not even go there."

"I'm not the one who opened the door."

"My mistake," she admitted graciously. "Let's just forget I mentioned it, okay?"

"Sure," he agreed, but it was too late.

He was already imagining her in a black silk G-string and spike heels, strutting her stuff to the pulsating beat of a live rock band. And Jim had an exceptionally vivid imagination. He didn't even have to close his eyes to conjure up the show.

She'd be small and sleek all over, the rest of her compact little body as well toned as her slender arms and smooth shoulders. Her breasts would be small, too, but exquisitely shaped, with pretty pink nipples the exact color of her lips. Her skin would be tantalizingly pale against the triangle of black silk between her legs.

Shifting in his seat, he was thankful for the solid tabletop that hid his erection from her. He reached for his beer and nearly drained his glass in an effort to cool the sudden heat of his body. It didn't do any good. He could still see her in that black G-string, her lithe torso undulating to a primitive jungle beat, her breasts swaying, her narrow hips rotating over his as she performed a private lap dance. He blinked hard, trying to dispel the image, and set the half-empty mug on the table.

"So." He reached down surreptitiously to adjust the front of his jeans before they cut off the blood supply to a very important part of his anatomy. "You said you had three kids," he said, looking for something—anything—to distract him from the lewd and lascivious pictures forming in his head. "How come you didn't have to rush home to them after work?"

"Because they're not here. The two youngest, Christopher and Emily, are spending the summer up at Moose Lake with my father. Kyle, my eighteen-year-old, is spending the summer in California with *their* father."

"Messy divorce, huh?" Jim said, picking up on her tone of voice.

"No, actually, it wasn't. It was kind of cold-blooded. Very efficient, in fact."

"What happened?"

"He went off on a business trip with his secretary. I didn't realize he wasn't coming back until I got the letter telling me where to send his things."

"You're kidding!" Jim couldn't believe any man could be that cold-blooded. "Jeez, you're not kidding! He actually expected you to pack up his belongings and send them to him?"

"The worst part is that I did it. Exactly as he instructed in the letter, down to the last detail." She couldn't help but smile at the incredulous look on Jim's face. "I was a different woman back then. More..." she lifted one shoulder in a little shrug and took a quick sip of beer, trying to find the right word to describe the woman she'd been; only one would do. "I was a doormat," she admitted.

"You've changed, then."

"Oh, yes," she agreed with a smile. "I've changed. I had to, to survive."

"It must have been hard."

"It was necessary," she said, and decided they'd talked about her long enough. Her story was boring and uninspired—the same sad story far too many women had to tell. "How about you?" she said, turning the tables. "How'd you end up wearing a hard hat?"

"I had a uncle in the business," he said easily. "I spent every summer vacation from ninth grade on working for him."

"Ah..." Andie nodded sagely. That was the way a lot

of guys got started. They had an uncle or a cousin or a father in the business, ready, willing and able to give them a place to start. "Nepotism."

"You got it."

"How come you're not with him now?"

"He retired a few years ago. Sold the business and moved to Florida."

"No sons to leave it to?"

"Nope. And before you ask, I wasn't interested in buying him out. Not then, anyway. And later, well..." He shrugged and left it at that.

Andie thought about the scars Dot had seen and the accident Jim didn't want to talk about and wondered what he was leaving out.

"Have you ever been married?" she asked, instead of delving into something that was obviously still a sore subject. But she really wanted to know.

"Nope."

"Engaged?"

"Nope."

"Ever lived with anyone?"

"I had a roommate once, while I was still at the aca— ah, when I first moved away from home. Does that count?"

"Female?"

"Nope."

"Then it doesn't count," Andie said with an decisive shake of her head. "The civilizing process doesn't start until you've actually lived with a woman."

"You're forgetting the three sisters."

"Oh, yes, the three sisters. All older, I think you said?" Andie considered for a moment. "Okay, sisters count." She leaned back, allowing the waiter to put their hamburgers and a basket of french-fried onion rings on the table. "Are you close to your family?" she asked, when the waiter had gone away again.

"Yeah, pretty close." Jim lifted the top bun off of his hamburger and began smearing it with spicy brown mustard. "We all get together for birthdays and holidays and the occasional Sunday dinner—things like that. Usually it's at my oldest sister Janet's house, now that the folks have retired and joined my uncle and his wife down in Florida. She and her husband have a big, rambling old place in Edina with kids and dogs and a big vegetable garden in the backyard." He screwed the top back on the mustard and set it aside. "She's into the whole earth-mother, domestic-goddess thing. You know—PTA, car pool, soccer practice, swimming lessons." He said it without a trace of sarcasm. In fact, he said it with more than a hint of pride and admiration in his voice. "She's real good at it, too. She's raising great kids."

"And your other sisters?" Andie reached for an onion ring and nibbled on the edge of it while she watched his hands and fantasized. "What do they do?"

"Jessie's a hotshot corporate lawyer with a fancy downtown office." He put the top bun back on his hamburger, flattened it a little with his palm, then lifted the whole thing to his mouth with both hands. "And Julie's a cop."

"A cop? Really? My dad's a cop. Or was. He retired last year from the Minneapolis police force. Maybe they know each other?"

Jim almost choked on a too-big bite of his hamburger. "I doubt it," he mumbled when he finally managed to swallow. "Julie's on the Eden Prairie police force."

"Well, you never know." Andie picked up a knife and neatly cut her hamburger in two. "Dad was a cop for nearly forty years. He knows a lot of people, on a lot of police forces all across Minnesota." She lifted one-half of her hamburger in both hands and then held it there, halfway between her mouth and the plate. "Come to think of it, Natalie might know her, too. She might even know your other sister, the lawyer. Nat's a private investigator," she told him. "She does a lot of work for lawyers all around the Twin Cities area. I'll have to remember to ask her next time I talk to her." She smiled at him over her hamburger. "Small world, isn't it?" she mused, and took a dainty bite of her sandwich.

"Small world," Jim agreed.

Thank God she had no idea *how* small.

He'd actually forgotten her father was a cop. Forgotten, too, that the sleek, sophisticated sister was a private investigator, all because he'd let himself get distracted by a vision of that sweet, sexy little body gyrating naked around a pole. Dammit, he knew sex would only get in the way! And he'd been right, as usual. It was time to get back to business, back to doing what he'd agreed to do. He picked up what was left of his beer and drained it in one long gulp, setting the heavy glass mug back down on the table with a sharp click.

Andie looked up at the sound and smiled at him over her hamburger. "You were right. It's good," she said, and took another dainty bite.

He waited until she was busy chewing before he asked his question. "Do you have any idea who's been vandalizing your job site?"

Andie's eyes widened, then narrowed almost imperceptibility in the time it took her to swallow what was in her mouth. "Who says anyone's been vandalizing the job site?"

"Just about everybody who works for you. It's a major topic of conversation."

She stared at him, dumbfounded. She'd had no idea her crew had been discussing her problems behind her back.

"I don't know why you're so surprised. People love to gossip. Especially about their bosses."

"What—"

"Can I get you folks anything else?" the waiter asked. He gestured at the empty glass in front of Jim. "Another beer?"

Andie shook her head impatiently and waved him away.

"That'll be all, thanks," Jim said politely, delaying the moment when he'd have to answer her question. "Just the check."

The waiter nodded and dug their bill out of his apron. "Pay at the bar," he said, as he laid it on the table.

"What do they say?" Andie asked again.

"Just that some graffiti artist has been leaving destructive tokens of his affection around the job site for the last month or so."

"Affection?"

"Figure of speech." Jim reached out and nudged her hand with the backs of his fingers. "Finish your hamburger before it gets cold," he said, waiting until she bit into it before he continued. "Dot said he quit for almost a week there, but then it started again this morning."

His inflection made it a question, and Andie nodded obediently, confirming what Dot had told him.

"I take it his latest effort involved all that red paint I saw smeared across the wall in the foyer?"

Andie nodded again.

"Is that all he does? Just spray paint around?"

Andie's hesitation was almost imperceptible. He would have missed it if he hadn't been watching her so closely. "Yes," she said.

"Are you sure?"

"Yes, of course, I'm sure." She put her hamburger down. "Why are you asking all these questions?" she demanded. "What's it to you?"

"I'm working for you now," he said smoothly, without missing a beat. "Which puts me in the line of fire, so to speak. I like to know what I'm up against."

"*You* aren't up against anything. I am. And it isn't anything, anyway." She was suddenly as prickly as a hedgehog. And as defensive as someone with something to hide. "Dot and the rest of them are making mountains out of molehills."

"If you say so," Jim said blandly, reaching out to pat the small clenched fist that lay by her plate.

"I say so." She threw off his hand with an impatient flick of her wrist. "And stop patronizing me. I detest being patronized."

"I'm sorry. I didn't mean to sound patronizing, I just meant—"

"I know what you meant," she snapped. "'Silly little woman,' is what you meant. 'Poor thing doesn't have a clue about what's going on or what to do about it,' is what you meant. 'She obviously needs someone to look after her,' is what you meant."

He shrugged, unwilling to admit that she'd pegged

it—and him—so neatly. But it hadn't sounded patronizing the way he'd said it. Had it?

"I suppose your next move is going to be an offer to help me with my little problem, isn't it?"

He shrugged again, tacitly admitting the truth of what she'd said and wondering why it made him feel guilty. What was so bad about offering to help? Even if he did have an ulterior motive.

"Maybe you'll use your contacts to nose around and find out who's behind it? Put a stop to it that way, or—no, I know! You'll catch him in the act! And, of course, I'll be expected to coo and flutter my eyelashes and tell you what a big, strong, important man you are." Andie pressed both hands to her chest like an old-fashioned dime-novel heroine and demonstrated. "No, thanks, I've—"

"Contacts?" he said carefully. What did she know about his contacts?

"—been in the construction business for nine years and I've got plenty of contacts of my own, if I need them."

Well, that answered the question of what she meant about his contacts.

"Which I don't," she said emphatically. "I can handle my 'little problem' without any well-meaning interference from you or any other man!"

There was a long moment of silence as they sat there, staring at each other over the remains of their dinner.

Jim cleared his throat. "Well," he said. "I guess I should at least be grateful you gave me the benefit of the doubt. Well-meaning," he added when she just looked at him. "You said you didn't need any well-meaning interference. And it *was* well-meaning," he said earnestly. "I was only trying to help."

"And?"

"And it was also patronizing. I'm sorry, I didn't mean to be. I won't make the same mistake again." He placed his hand, palm up, on the table between them. "Friends?"

Andie hesitated, torn by conflicting emotions. He was a supremely macho male animal, with all the faults that label implied. He was arrogant, cocky and domineering, with a sure and certain belief in the rightness of his own viewpoint and the strong conviction that he knew best—especially when it came to dealing with the so-called weaker sex. On the other hand, he'd been a charming dinner companion up until he'd started sticking his nose where it didn't belong. But then he'd apologized, as nice as you please, and admitted he'd been wrong and committed himself to trying to do better and...and, darn it, he had the most beautiful mouth she'd ever seen on a man! Right now it was quirked up at one corner in a little half smile that made her insides all warm and quivery.

"From here on out, I won't offer you any advice or help unless you specifically ask for it." That little half smile became a self-mocking grin. "Well, I'll *try* not to offer any advice. Okay?"

Andie melted.

What did it matter if he was arrogant and domineering? He had no control over her. He didn't hold any position of authority or influence in her life. Nor would he ever. She wasn't planning to marry the man. She wasn't even planning on dating him. She was just planning to...to...

She was just planning to go to bed with him, she realized.

Tonight.

She reached out and put her hand in his. "Friends," she said softly, with a smile that made him wonder what she was up to.

5

IT WAS SURPRISINGLY EASY to get him to go home with her. She merely reminded him, in a casual aside as they were walking out to their vehicles in the darkened parking lot, that she was heading home to an empty house. He gallantly offered to follow her and see that she arrived safely. She demurred, saying it wasn't necessary, and he—predictably—insisted. There were, it seemed, some definite advantages in dealing with a macho male. Arrogant and domineering they might be, but their protective instincts operated in overdrive, making them easy to handle if one used the right approach. It was a fact Andie was only just now beginning to appreciate, though her sister had been trying to impress that particular reality on her for some time. She should have listened to Natalie.

"Looks like I owe you an apology, Nat," she murmured, glancing into her rearview mirror as she turned into the driveway of her dark, silent house.

True to his word, Jim Nicolosi was right on her tail. She could see the single headlight of his big black Harley Davidson as he turned in behind her and came to a stop. The muted roar of the bike's engine was a deep, rhythmic growl, a pulsating sound she could feel as well as hear. It seemed to travel beneath the pavement of her driveway and up through the tires of her ancient Chevy pickup, creating vibrations that resonated throughout her body. Or maybe it was just the wild beating of her heart that was making her insides quiver.

He cut the bike's engine, and she was abruptly surrounded by the silence of a quiet residential street on a quiet Minnesota summer night. Definitely her heart. Her insides were still quivering and she pressed a hand against her chest. Her heart was pounding out an unfamiliar rhythm that was almost frightening in its intensity.

Yet she wanted everything she was due.

And she wanted it with this man.

She curled her fingers around the door handle of the truck and pushed, shouldering the door open just as Jim pulled on it from the outside. She tumbled into his arms in an artless heap.

"Sorry," she said, glancing up at him from under her lashes.

"No problem," he said, looking as if he expected her to jerk away from him.

She didn't so much as tense a muscle.

COMPLICATIONS, Jim reminded himself sternly as every cell in his body went on full alert. He couldn't afford any complications. And she'd made it more than plain that she wasn't interested, anyway. Well, okay, she *was* interested, he amended. He could always tell when a woman was interested. But she'd let him know, albeit indirectly, that she didn't want the complications any more than he did. He put his hands on her bare arms, the way he had earlier that evening, and set her firmly on her own two feet.

She hesitated, as if reluctant to move away from him, and he realized she must be frightened and unwilling to admit it. No matter how tough she acted or what she said to the contrary, she had to be upset by what was going on at the job site. Any woman would be. Except maybe his sister Julie, the tough-as-nails cop. "Would you like me to come in and turn on a few lights for you?" he asked.

Andie couldn't believe seduction was really going to be this easy. "Would you mind?" she murmured a little breathlessly.

"No problem," he said again, and took her by the hand. He led her across the pebbled path she'd laid down through the lawn last summer and up the steps to the front of the little clapboard house. "Key?" he said, holding out his hand.

Andie pressed it into his palm, then stood aside while Jim opened the door and reached inside to turn on the light. When he'd crossed the threshold he stepped back and held the door open for her.

"Wait here a minute while I take a quick look around," he ordered, and headed upstairs.

Andie's first instinct was to do as she was told and wait.

Which was exactly why she didn't.

She went into the kitchen instead, walking down the dark center hallway toward the back of the house without a flicker of nervousness. Flipping on the overhead light, she glanced at the answering machine and was relieved to see that the red light wasn't blinking. That meant the kids hadn't called. And neither, thank goodness, had anyone else. She'd been getting some disturbing calls lately, of the heavy-breather variety. One of those tonight would probably spoil the mood.

"Andrea?"

"In the kitchen," she hollered. "Straight back down the hall to your right. I decided a cup of coffee sounded good," she said, smiling at Jim as he entered the room. "Would you like some? It'll only take a few minutes to brew."

Complications, he reminded himself again. *Complications*. The situation was rife with them. A man and a woman. Late at night. All alone in an empty house. They could get into serious trouble without half trying.

"I probably ought to be going," he said, without much conviction. "It's getting late, and I've got to be up early tomorrow." He flashed her a teasing grin. "I've got a tough new boss who'll dock my pay if I'm tardy."

"One cup?" she wheedled. "To say thanks for seeing me home? I promise to put in a good word with your boss."

"All right." What could one cup of coffee hurt? "One cup."

Andie turned away to hide her smile of satisfaction at his easy capitulation. Easy, this was going to be so easy! She wondered why in the world she'd ever been nervous. There was nothing to this game of seduction. "Why don't you go on into the family room and make yourself comfortable? I'll bring the coffee in when it's ready. Go on," she said, flapping a hand at him when he hesitated. "There's a CD player and a stack of CDs in the bookcase. Pick out something soothing."

She had an eclectic taste in music. Willie Nelson shared shelf space with Mary Chapin Carpenter, George Jones, Pasty Cline, Mozart, Chopin and an impressive collection of rock 'n' roll artists from the mid-fifties to the early seventies. There were also a couple of CDs by Nine Inch Nails and Nirvana, but he figured it was a good bet those belonged to the eighteen-year-old son. Jim ran his fingers over the selection of discs, foregoing rock 'n' roll in favor of Chopin. No way did he want to listen to Mick Jagger whine about the difficulty of finding "Satisfaction" or Rod Stewart croak out "Tonight's the Night" when there was no satisfaction in sight and it most definitely *wasn't* the night. Besides, she'd said soothing, hadn't she? And what was Chopin if not soothing? The soft strains of a piano concerto had just starting drifting through the room when the lights suddenly flickered and dimmed.

"There, that's better, isn't it?" Andie said, when he turned to see what had caused the lights to malfunction. "So much more soothing than all that glare."

There was that word again, he thought. *Soothing.* Yet here he was, feeling anything but soothed.

"Feel free to get comfortable," she invited, flashing a quick smile at him. "Sit down. Put your feet up. The furniture in here is impervious to just about everything." She placed the tray she carried on the waxed pine coffee table in front of the sofa and sat, curling one bare foot under her. The tray was natural wicker with a pale blue napkin spread across it. The cups were delicate white china with tiny blue flowers on them. There was also a small plate of cookies—*biscotti*, he thought they were called—and a crystal decanter with two snifters.

"Sit," she said, patting the cushion next to her when he continued to stand there, staring down at her.

Jim sat.

"Would you like your brandy in your coffee or alongside it?" she asked, as she leaned forward to reach for the decanter.

And the lightbulb finally clicked on in his head.

The dim lights. The soft music. The invitation to make himself comfortable. The way she had made *herself* comfortable by taking off her shoes. The brandy.

It was a scene straight out of one of those old Rock Hudson/Doris Day movies, where perennial-virgin Doris was about to get herself compromised. Only, unless he was very much mistaken, *he* was playing the part of the unwitting virgin.

He reached out, covering her hand with his, trapping her fingers against the decanter, stopping her from lifting it from the tray.

A thrill zinged through Andie and she went stockstill, waiting for him to make his move. *Aching* for him to make it.

"Are you by any chance trying to seduce me?"

She flushed and bit her lip. Maybe this wasn't going to be quite as easy as she'd thought, after all. She hadn't counted on having to explain it to him. She'd assumed he'd get the hint eventually and just take over from there.

"Andrea?" He let go of her hand and slowly—oh, so slowly—ran his fingers up her arm and across her shoulder to her chin. Gently, with just the tip of one callused finger, he turned her to face him.

She kept her gaze lowered.

"Look at me," he ordered softly.

Andie obediently raised her eyes to his.

"Well, I'll be damned," he said, when he saw what was in them. "You *are* trying to seduce me."

"What if I am?"

"Well..." One corner of his beautiful mouth turned up in a teasing little smile. "I could protest and say I'm not that kind of guy, but..."

"But?" she whispered.

"We'd both know I'd be lying through my teeth."

"Then your virtue's not all it should be? Is that what you're telling me?"

"Definitely not all it should be."

"And you're corruptible?"

"Oh, without a doubt."

"Well, then...?" She leaned closer, just a tiny bit closer to that beautiful, tempting mouth. Her eyes drifted closed as she waited for his kiss.

"Just one question," he murmured, delaying the inevitable for one delicious moment longer.

Andie sighed and opened her eyes. "What?"

"Will you still respect me in the morning?"

She gave a soft gurgle of delighted laughter. "I'd say that depends on how well you do tonight," she said, and pressed her lips to his, unable to wait even one moment longer to taste him.

She didn't have to tell him what to do after that. He knew.

He slid his hand from her chin to the side of her face, splaying his fingers in the soft hair at her temples, cupping her cheek in his callused palm, rubbing his thumb lightly back and forth over the curve of her jaw as his lips took hers. She couldn't have said how long the kiss went on, seconds or minutes or hours, but it was everything a kiss should be. Soft and delicate one moment, gently coaxing a response. Hard and heated the next, ruthlessly demanding. His lips plucked at hers, then plundered. His tongue teased, then took. He was infinitely soothing, then unbearably exciting.

Finally, he raised his head and looked into her eyes. By this time the two of them were lying on the sofa, her body pressed deep into the blue plaid cushions by the weight of his. His lean hips were nestled between her slender thighs. His chest was pressed against her giving breasts. His fingers were tangled in the soft, wispy strands of her hair. They were both flushed and warm. Both breathing more heavily than normal. Both aching with anticipation and need.

Jim raised himself onto his elbows. "Are you sure about this?" he murmured.

Andie nodded. Yes, she was sure, except... "I'm not on any kind of birth control," she said, shy but determined to be a modern woman. And a modern woman took responsibility. "But I've got some, uh..."

"So do I." He grinned wickedly. "Never leave home without 'em."

"Oh, well, in that case..." Andie smiled and flexed her hips, rolling them up to meet the instant, instinctive thrust of his as she moved beneath him. And then she placed her small, work-worn hands on either side of his face. "Shut up and kiss me," she said, and pulled his mouth back down to hers.

"Yes, ma'am," Jim murmured huskily, and did as he was told.

He slid one arm around her and under her, cradling her head in his hand as he slid the other down to knead the small, soft mound of her breast, all the while giving her more of the kisses she craved. Soft kisses. Sweet kisses. Deep and light, and fast and slow. Tiny, tender butterfly kisses against her cheeks and nose and the lids of her eyes. Damp, openmouthed baby kisses against her throat. Wet, panting, suctioning kisses when he finally bared her breast and took her nipple into his mouth.

Andie moaned and arched beneath him, inviting more, asking for more, *demanding* more. She wanted it all. Now. Everything he had to give. Everything there was. Everything she had been denying herself for longer than her starved body could remember. Her hips pumped sensuously against his, undulating, rotating, seeking to put the hard ridge of his erection where she needed it most. She was like wildfire in his arms, quivering uncontrollably, her whole slender body trembling with intemperate passion and mindless, aching need. He could feel the incredible heat and moistness of her through two layers of heavy denim.

"Take it easy, sweetheart," he murmured, trying to soothe her. "Take it easy. We've got all night to get there."

She curled her fingers in his thick, silky hair. "*Now,*" she demanded, and yanked. Hard. "*Now, now, now!*"

It was a plea he couldn't ignore. Or resist. He levered himself up off of her, sliding to his knees on the floor by the sofa. She whimpered and reached out blindly, feverishly, clutching at the fabric of his T-shirt to pull him back on top of her. He evaded her seeking hands and deftly unhooked the remaining strap of her overalls and the row of metal buttons down one side. Grasping the heavy material in both hands, he peeled her out of it, leaving the dusty, paint-stained overalls in a heap on the floor. She wore cotton bikini panties underneath, white with tiny pink flowers, and a plain white tank-style T-shirt. The T-shirt was twisted up under her arms, pushed there when he'd bared her breasts for his mouth. The panties were cut high on her thighs and low across her stomach, revealing all but her most intimate secrets. He reached out to touch her reverently, running his fingertips over her long legs and smooth, well-defined thighs; her slender hips and flat stomach; her small, perfect breasts with their tightly puckered pink nipples. He would have taken more time with his caresses, he would have lingered to fondle and tickle and tease before going further, but she grabbed his hand in both of hers and thrust it between her legs.

"Touch me."

With a strangled oath, Jim curled his fingers and cupped her. The heat was incredible. Incendiary. Scorching. He moved his fingers over the sopping cotton, lightly stroking her. She cried out as the first climax rolled through her, lifting her hips for more.

"Please," she murmured brokenly. "Oh, please."

She was so hot, so needy, that once wasn't going to be nearly enough.

Jim curled his fingers over the elastic waistband of her panties, dragged them ruthlessly down her legs and tossed them over his shoulder. They'd barely floated down to settle on top of the discarded overalls before he had her twisted around into a sitting position on the sofa, with her legs spread-eagled and his hands pressed against the inside of her sleek, muscled thighs to hold them open. The soft folds between her legs were swollen with passion, slick with need, weeping. He pulled her closer to the edge of the sofa and opened her wider, using his thumbs to expose the tiny nubbin of tender flesh hidden between her legs. And then he bent his head and took her with his mouth.

Andie shrieked and reared up, but he put one hand in the middle of her chest and pushed her back down, holding her there until she screamed again...and then again...and yet again. And then, when she was weak from release, spent and panting and sobbing, he reached down and unbuttoned his jeans, freeing his erection.

Knowing she wasn't going to go anywhere, that she didn't even have the energy to move, he let go of her and used two hands to quickly sheath his penis in one of the condoms he kept handy in the fifth pocket of his jeans. That done, he dragged her hips over the edge of the sofa, slid his hands under her buttocks to position her and drove himself into her to the hilt.

She came again, immediately, with a white-hot burst of passion that brought her back arching up off the sofa and pressed her head into it. Her wild response triggered his. He managed one thrust...two...three...and then exploded. The force of it threw his head back and his hips forward, and left fingerprint-size bruises in the soft flesh of her buttocks. It seemed to go on and on, draining him, wringing him dry, scorching him from the top of his head to the soles of his feet. And when it was over, it took all the remaining strength he possessed to lift her hips back onto the sofa before he collapsed in a heap and pitched forward, face first, onto her lap.

They rested quietly for a few minutes. Jim was on his knees in front of the sofa, still completely dressed, with his jeans and Jockey shorts sagging down around his lean hips. Andie lay sprawled beneath him, naked except for the T-shirt twisted up under her arms and the whisker burn on her thighs. Both of them were breathing deeply, struggling to catch their breath and calm their rampaging hearts.

Jim recovered first and raised his head, giving her a

quizzical look from beneath a lifted brow. "That wasn't just me," he said.

Andie returned his look with a blank stare, not understanding.

"I'm good," he said, as he hauled himself up from the floor and flopped down beside her on the sofa, "but I'm not that good."

Andie turned her head to smile at him. "You were wonderful."

"Oh, without a doubt," he agreed with a cocky grin. "But that's not what I meant. You were primed and ready before I even touched you." He reached over and brushed her nipple lightly with the back of one finger. It beaded instantly, drawing up into a hard little nub. "You're ready for another round right now."

Embarrassed, Andie reached up with both hands and pulled down her T-shirt, pushing his hand away and covering her telltale response. "It's been awhile."

"Awhile," he repeated, and lowered his hand, skimming his knuckle back and forth over the tuft of silky blond hair at the apex of her thighs. "How long is awhile?"

Andie felt the muscles in her thighs begin to quiver again. "A few years."

"Years?" Well aware of her response, Jim turned his hand over and rested it there, palm down. "As in more than one?"

"Yes."

"More than two?" He began to stroke her, very softly, with one finger.

"Yes," she said, and closed her eyes.

"Three?"

"Ah..." She sucked in her breath as his finger dipped lower.

"More than three?" he persisted.

"Yes...yes, more than three."

"How many more?"

"Ah...mmm...oh, that feels so good...I...eight."

"Eight?" His hand stilled. "You haven't had sex in *eight years?*"

"Yes," she said, and bit down on her bottom lip to keep from whimpering.

"Oh, you poor baby," he crooned, shocked to his very core. "No wonder you're so hungry." He turned and grasped her by the waist with both hands, dragging her across his lap so that she sat facing him, with her legs straddling his. "Here, let's get this out of the way," he said, reaching for the hem of her T-shirt.

She raised her arms, like a child being undressed for bed, and let him pull it over her head. It joined the rest of her clothes on the floor.

He cupped her breasts in his palms, plumping them. "Such pretty little things," he said, and kissed each pouting pink nipple. He slid his hands down, over her rib cage and the inward curve of her waist. "Such a pretty little body." And down, cresting the gentle swell of her hips, skimming the outside of her legs to her knees, and back up again, with his fingers spread, trailing his thumbs along the sensitive flesh of her inner thighs to her vulva. "Such a pretty little—"

She flushed pink with embarrassment and pressed her fingers to his mouth, stopping him before he could say it.

"Well, it is," he insisted, and reached up, capturing her hand. Holding her gaze with his, he sucked each of her fingers into his mouth, slowly, wetting them thoroughly, then took her hand and pressed it down between her splayed thighs. "Feel how pretty you are," he said.

She squirmed and whimpered, and finally acquiesced, throwing her head back as he used her own fingers to pleasure her.

"That's it...ah, yes, that's it," he murmured, his eyes avid and hot as he watched her find release. She was wild again, hips rotating to the primitive beat of the hot blood pounding through her veins, breasts swaying seductively, her breath coming in short, gasping pants as she unwittingly performed a very private lap dance for an enthralled audience of one. He let go of her hand after a minute, unable to bear it any longer, and sheathed himself in a second condom. Then he grasped her wildly gyrating hips in both hands and guided her down onto his straining erection.

She gasped and clutched at his shoulders, curling her fingers into the fabric of his T-shirt to steady herself as he slowly, inexorably, filled her.

"Easy now, baby. Easy. Pace yourself," he instructed, as she began to move on him. "You've got a lot of catching up to do."

THEY NEVER DID GET to the coffee. It sat untouched, cooling in the pretty china cups on the wicker tray on the waxed pine coffee table, while they used the brandy to paint each other in strategic and interesting places. They made love on the floor on the colorful hooked rug, with Andie on top, driving Jim crazy while she caressed her own breasts and slowly rode him to oblivion. They made love draped over the back of the sofa, with Jim behind her, his hands around and under her body, caressing her breasts while he pounded into her like a jackhammer. They made love on the stairs, with Andie clinging to the balusters. And in the shower, up against the tiled wall, with tepid water beating down on their overheated bodies. And on the bed, where it was Jim's turn to writhe and moan and plead while she pleasured him with her mouth.

They made love all through the night, with laughter and tenderness, with languid ease and wild, unrestrained ferocity, with imagination and heat and greedy, unbridled passion until, finally, somewhere in the wee small hours of the morning, they were simply too spent to move and fell into a tumbled, exhausted heap on the disordered bed.

6

ANDIE'S USUALLY TRUSTY internal alarm clock failed her
the next morning. She awoke, briefly, in the misty gray
predawn hours when Jim crept from the bed and began
to dress in the dark. "Go back to sleep," he murmured
when she roused, and she obediently snuggled into her
pillows and drifted off into delicious dreams of the
night before. She came fully awake several hours later
with a start and a muffled curse when a narrow band of
sunlight sneaked through the bedroom curtains and
touched her face.

It was almost nine o'clock.

FOR THE FIRST TIME in a very long time, Andie was late
for work. And everyone else—*everyone*—was on time.

The sight of Jim's gleaming black Harley, parked in
the street behind Dot's beat-up, vintage Volkswagen
van, had her pressing a hand to her stomach, trying to
calm the emotions that started it roiling at the thought
of facing him in the bright light of the morning after.
Anticipation. Eagerness. Embarrassment. Dread. Their
first meeting this morning was bound to be excruciatingly awkward.

Last night, she'd been naked in his arms. She'd done
things with him and to him and for him that she'd never
done before—not even during her eleven-year marriage to the father of her children. Last night, she'd

come truly, completely alive. She'd discovered and reveled in a part of herself she'd been denying for far too long. And yet this morning she fully intended to treat him as if none of it had ever happened, as if he was simply a man who happened to work for her. No matter that she wore the marks of his passion everywhere on her body.

Her inner thighs were still red and deliciously tender from the scrape of his stubbled jaw. There was a series of tiny purple bruises on each hip from the force of his grip. A sucker bite adorned her right breast. She ached in places she'd almost forgotten she had. And she felt absolutely marvelous.

Earlier that morning, when she'd looked in the mirror at the wisps of blond hair sticking up all over her head, at her puffy lips and glowing skin and heavy eyes, she'd thought she looked pretty darn marvelous, in spite of her trepidation over how she had spent the night. Now she was afraid that everybody was going to take one look at her and *know*.

How do men do it? she wondered, thinking of the way her ex-husband had treated the woman who had been both his secretary and his lover. Not even his ex-partner had known they were having an affair until the two of them ran off together. Everything had been so normal until then, so routine. Maybe that was the secret. Maybe the way to handle the situation was to take a page out of Kevin's book and pretend there was no secret.

She forced herself to get out of her truck without hurrying, to stand in the open V of the door and buckle on her tool belt as she did every morning. Forced herself to lean in and pick up her big silver thermos by its red plastic handle as if it didn't still have yesterday's cold, stale coffee in it; to cross the street and walk up the brick walkway as if it was nothing out of the ordinary for her to arrive at the job site at twenty minutes to ten in the morning with a hickey hidden under the blue bandanna knotted ever so casually around her neck.

"Morning, Dan," she said to the stonemason, who was standing in front of the house. He was busily directing his crew as they erected scaffolding around the tower in preparation for refurbishing and restoring the richly patterned brickwork that decorated it. "How's it going?"

"Doesn't look like this'll need as much work as I first thought. Needs a good cleaning and a coupla bricks replaced here and there, little daub of mortar to hold it all together, and that'll do it." He smacked the patterned brick wall with the flat of his hand. "They don't build 'em like this anymore."

"No, they don't," Andie agreed with a smile. Less work meant less time and less money, which was always good news to a contractor. And he hadn't mentioned her tardiness. Maybe be no one else would notice, either.

Yeah, right.

The rest of her crew was more familiar with her normal routine than Dan Johnston was. And few of them would pass up the chance to razz the boss if the opportunity presented itself. Andie squared her shoulders and walked up the steps to the open front door. The sooner she faced it, the better.

"Heads up," Booker warned as he slipped in the door behind her carrying a twelve-by-four-foot panel of Sheetrock.

Andie smiled at the young man. Here was one employee who wouldn't razz her about anything. It was all he could do to string two sentences together in her presence. She wasn't sure if it was her gender or her position as his boss that tied his tongue in knots, but right now she was grateful for small favors, for whatever reason.

"I took a look at the rooms on the third floor before I left last night," she said, casting a quick glance around as Booker placed the unwieldy panel with those already stacked against the open stringer of the grand staircase. No graffiti marred the newly plastered walls, nor was her lover with the slow hands in sight. She wondered where he was, and then told herself she didn't care. She'd assigned him to Dot; his whereabouts on the job was Dot's responsibility. What happened last night wasn't going to change anything in that department. It wasn't going to change anything at all, period. "You're doing a real nice job in the servants' bathroom, Booker."

The young man flashed her a quick, pleased smile. "Gee, thanks," he said, flushing at the compliment.

"When you finish it up, let me know," she said, as he started out the front door to get another panel. "I'd like you to give me a hand in the master bath as soon as you're free."

That stopped the young apprentice in his tracks. *"Thanks,"* he said again, with gusto, but she'd already turned and headed off across the room, unaware that he stood staring after her with a dazzled expression on his face.

She discovered Pete Lindstrom, journeyman carpenter, in the gutted parlor, using a table saw to cut trim. He raised his head as she passed through the room and gave her a solemn nod. She nodded back, smiling a quick greeting, indicating that he should keep on with what he was doing as she hurried through the room.

She found Mary Free in the dining room, standing at the foot of a tall ladder, watching Tiffany as she carefully removed the ornate plaster rose in the middle of the ceiling in preparation for installing a new electrical box behind it for the chandelier. Mary, the master electrician, glanced around as Andie entered the room.

"We got that shipment of hand-painted tiles you've been waiting for," she said by way of greeting. "It came about half an hour ago."

"The tile came?" All thoughts of her tardiness—and the tall, dark, handsome reason for it—vanished from Andie's mind for a brief moment. She'd been expecting that tile for weeks and had expected to wait weeks more. "Where is it?"

"Upstairs," Mary said, reaching with both hands for the plaster rose that Tiffany handed her. "Dot said to let you know it was here as soon as you came in."

"She also said you told her not to let me have more than one Screaming Orgasm last night," Tiffany complained as she slipped her screwdriver into its slot on her tool belt and reached for the needle-nose pliers. "Said you were afraid I'd end up like you if I did."

"Excuse me?" Andie murmured, as visions of her own screaming orgasms—many more than just one—suddenly replayed themselves in her head.

"A mother," Tiffany said, and grinned at her own cleverness. "You know—orgasms...pregnancy tests... babies..." she explained when Andie just stared at her. "Put them all together and what have you got?"

"Oh. A mother. Of course," she said, managing a

small smile at the joke in spite of the way her insides clenched.

Oh, God, I hope not!

She and Jim had used condoms each and every time last night to prevent just such an occurrence. He'd had only two in the pocket of his jeans, but fortunately, Andie had been able to supply the others that were needed, thanks to the open box of Trojans she'd found in her son's dresser drawer when she was cleaning his room after he'd left for California.

She'd been appalled—shocked at the evidence, as any mother of a teenager would be, that her son obviously had a sex life. For a while she'd been torn between relief at the thought that leaving his condoms behind meant he wasn't planning on having sex while he was out in California and worry that he had made a careless oversight that he—and some young girl—would end up paying for for the rest of their lives. Worry had finally won out. She'd called Kyle out in California and discussed the matter with him—much to the mutual embarrassment of both mother and son. She'd forgotten about the condoms hidden in her son's dresser drawer after that.

Until last night.

Last night she'd been reduced to raiding her teenage son's stash of prophylactics! It was probably immoral, and she would absolutely *die* of embarrassment if she ever had to account to him for the missing condoms, but that would be infinitely better than getting pregnant. As much as she loved being a mother, as much as she would love having another child, she simply wasn't in any position to do so. And certainly not with a man who was just a...just a...

She groped for a word, trying to find one that wouldn't make it sound as shameless as it was. There wasn't one. She, Andrea Wagner, a normally responsible mother of three, had had a fling with a man she barely knew. She had wantonly indulged in a one-night stand with a gorgeous young stud.

And enjoyed every blessed minute of it!

But it couldn't happen again.

It really couldn't.

At least, not until she'd laid down a few ground rules. And bought her own supply of condoms.

Good Lord, what was she thinking?

Of *course*, it couldn't happen again.

"You're looking kind of peaked, there, Andie," Tiffany said as she climbed down the ladder. "Maybe you should have stayed in bed a little longer this morning. Preferably with a man. A little morning nooky would put some color in those cheeks." Her grin was good-natured and cheerfully lascivious. "I know it always gets *my* blood pumping."

"Everything gets your blood pumping," Mary chided her.

Andie could only hope she wasn't blushing. "You said Dot is upstairs?" she asked Mary, without acknowledging Tiffany's comment.

"Uh-huh. She's got Ed up there waiting while she and Jim unpack both crates of tiles to make sure everything you ordered is there and intact."

"I guess I'd better go on up and take at look at it myself, then," Andie said.

The fact that Jim was upstairs, helping to unpack the tile, was completely beside the point. She wasn't going upstairs to see him; she was merely going about her usual business of ensuring the job—all the jobs—got done. It would be unusual if she *didn't* go upstairs to check on the tile herself. Nothing had changed. She wasn't doing anything differently just because they'd slept together. She was still the boss, still in charge.

"Andie really does look kind of tired this morning, don't you think?" she heard Tiffany say as she headed out of the dining room and back toward the front hall. "Do you think she's all right?"

"She's been working too hard. Dot says she—" Mary began, but the whine of Pete's saw coming from the parlor drowned out the rest.

But Andie had heard enough to have her hesitating at the bottom of the staircase with her foot on the first riser and her hand clutching the newel post.

Dot says...

Oh, Lord, what *would* Dot say?

She wasn't a lowly apprentice like Booker, who was afraid to express his opinion in front of his boss. She wasn't a self-absorbed hedonist like Tiffany. She wasn't quiet and reserved like Mary. Or taciturn and withdrawn like Pete. She was observant and outspoken. Moreover, she was a friend. And as a friend, she wouldn't hesitate to voice her opinion of a night spent indulging in wild, abandoned sex with a man one had known for less than two days. A man who was an employee, no less.

Andie was halfway afraid Dot would upbraid her for her foolishness, and halfway afraid she wouldn't.

Natalie and Dot both had often lamented the lack of a man in Andie's life. What if Dot didn't try to discourage her from turning this one-night stand into a full-fledged affair? What if she condoned it, instead? What if she encouraged Andie to go for it?

She'd been counting on Dot to talk some sense into her, she realized; she'd been relying on the older woman to point out all the reasons an affair with Jim Nicolosi wasn't a good idea. If Dot didn't try to talk her out of it, who would? Not Natalie, certainly. Her sister was the one who had put the idea into her head in the first place.

God knows, you're due, she'd said.

Well, Andie had certainly collected last night. In full. And then some.

Now what was she supposed to do?

"Just pretend it never happened," she murmured to herself, as she started up the stairs. "It never happened. It never happened. It never hap—"

She pulled up short, standing stock-still on the threshold of the sitting room, as suddenly breathless as if she had been punched in the stomach. She'd thought she'd been prepared. Last night was last night and today was something else entirely, and she was adult enough to separate the two. Except that just looking at him brought all kinds of feelings to the surface. And...*Lord, he was gorgeous!*

He was on his knees on the floor of the sitting room, in profile to the door. Sunlight from the large bay window on the east side of the room slanted across his broad back and one side of his face, it fell across his right shoulder to highlight the slow, careful movements of his hands as he dug through the crate in front of him. Dust motes—microscopic bits of drywall and marble—created a nimbus around his head that made him look almost magical, mythical, like a male Pandora opening the box that would loose joy and mischief on the world.

Andie blinked, trying to dispel the image. She told herself not to be ridiculous.

He was just a man doing a job.

And she was his boss.

There was nothing the least bit magical in that.

And then he lifted one of the tiles out of the crate and gently brushed off the bits of protective insulation clinging to it, smoothing his palm over the painted surface before he handed it to Dot. She, in turn, made a check mark on the bill of lading, then placed the tile on top of a long table made of a narrow panel of Sheetrock, two boards and a pair of sawhorses. The supplier stood to one side looking bored and put out, waiting for the moment when his paperwork was signed and he could leave.

All Andie could think about was the magic Jim had created last night when he had touched her with those very same hands, in that very same way, caressing her with his fingers, smoothing his palms over her body with delicacy and care and appreciation, as if she were as exquisite and fragile as a rare piece of porcelain. The same soul-deep thrill that had run through her then ran through her now, just thinking about it.

Pretending nothing had happened was going to be a lot harder than she'd thought. A *lot* harder. She took a quick breath, squared her shoulders and stepped into the room.

"Morning, everybody," she said brightly, including everyone—and no one in particular—in her smile. "Sorry I'm late." She crossed over to the makeshift table to view the tiles as if they were the only thing on her mind. "Oh, these are great."

Most of the tiles were small, four-inch squares, painted with yellow roses and green leaves that would look like intertwined vines when formed into a border at the baseboard, wainscot and cornice levels in the master bathroom. The most complex and expensive tiles were six-inch squares, painted so that when they were installed, the roses on them would be arranged in a single large bouquet tied with a pink ribbon.

"They look like they'll be a perfect match, don't they?" Andie picked up a tile, turning it to the sunlight to admire the exquisite detailing, which, not coincidentally, turned her away from Jim. "Is this all of them?" she asked Dot. "The entire order?"

"Seems to be." Dot looked at Jim for confirmation rather than the supplier.

"That's the last one," he said, gesturing toward the tile Andie still held.

Dot glanced down at the bill of lading in her hand. "Then that's it," she said. "Everything's here."

"Can I get this delivery receipt signed now?" Ed asked in an aggrieved voice. "I've got other deliveries to make today, you know."

Andie glanced at Dot.

"It's all in order," Dot said. "Not so much as a chip on any one of them."

Andie set the tile back on the table and took the delivery receipt from the supplier. "I'd like you to come downstairs and take a look at the delft tiles around the Aga stove in the kitchen before you leave," she said as she signed it. "If you've got time, that is," she added, knowing he would. Ed was from the old school. He didn't much like dealing with a woman, especially when she was the one making the decisions and giving the orders, but he managed to put aside his prejudices when money was involved. "I want to match the broken tiles with originals, if possible," Andie told him. "If not, we're going to need to replace them with reproductions."

"No problem." He took the receipt, gave her the customer copy and slipped the rest of the paperwork into a hard-sided document folder. "I've also got some catalogs from a couple of companies that specialize in delft reproductions if you want to come out to the van to take a look."

"Good. Let's do that right now, so you can get on your way, shall we? Dot, I'd like you to talk to Pete as soon as you can about the trim he's been cutting to finish that wainscoting in the hall. He should be about done with it," Andie said, starting for the door. "Oh, and, Jim..." she paused and turned around to look at him, without quite meeting his eyes. "I want you to repack all this tile. I think it'll be safer in the crates until we're ready to install it." She issued her orders as if he was just another apprentice who worked for her. "After that, you can finish with the mantelpiece in the master bedroom." She glanced at Dot. "Unless you have something else you want him to do today?"

Dot shook her head. "You're the boss."

Yes, Andie thought, as she led the supplier down the back stairs to the kitchen, *I am*. And she intended to keep it that way.

DOT CAUGHT UP WITH ANDIE thirty minutes later. She was sitting cross-legged on the floor of the cavernous kitchen, using a flat-head screwdriver to dismantle the pine skirt that enclosed the large porcelain sink and its attendant plumbing. "I wondered where you were hiding out," Dot said.

Andie didn't even pause to glance over her shoulder. "Excuse me?"

"I thought you were planning to start on the master bathroom today."

"I decided to wait until Booker is finished in the servants' bathroom." And until Jim was finished in the master bedroom. "I think he should be in on it from the beginning. He'll learn more that way."

"Uh-huh." Dot leaned back against the kitchen counter and crossed her arms. "What's going on?"

"Ed said he thinks we'll be able to replace the broken delft tiles without too much problem," Andie said, deliberately misunderstanding the question. "I wish I could say the same for this sink, but it's too badly cracked to be salvaged. The fixtures and hardware are in good condition, though. And this pine is in excellent shape. Once it's sanded and refinished it will be as good as new."

"Did he make a pass at you or something?"

"Who?" Andie dropped a screw into the plastic peanut-butter jar at her hip. "Ed?"

"No. Not Ed. We both know you're not his type. He likes his women a bit more compliant."

"Thank the Lord for small favors," Andie said fervently.

"Amen to that," Dot agreed. "So...did Jim make a pass at you or what?"

"Jim?" Andie tensed, but didn't stop working. "No,

of course not. What makes you even think such a thing?"

"You practically gave the poor guy frostbite. I figured he must have done something to deserve it."

"No." Andie focused all her attention on the screw she was twisting out of the wood. "He didn't do a thing." Except turn her inside out and upside down and...

"Did you make a pass at him?"

"No, I did n—ouch!" The screwdriver clattered to the floor as Andie rammed her knuckles against the wooden panel, scraping them against the half-exposed screw. "Now look what you made me do!" She raised her hand, licking at the thin line of blood that welled across her knuckles. "Jeez, I really gouged myself." She searched in her back pocket for her bandanna to staunch the blood.

"Around your neck," Dot said helpfully.

Without thinking, Andie reached up and loosened the blue bandanna. "Darn thing stings like the dickens," she said, as she dragged the scarf from around her neck and wrapped her hand.

"That's what you get for telling fibs."

Andie glanced up from under lowered lashes. "What's that supposed to mean?"

"It looks to me like somebody sure as hell made a pass at somebody."

Too late, Andie lifted her hand to cover the telltale mark on her neck.

"Did you sleep with him?"

She didn't even think about lying. "Yes," she said, and braced herself for the lecture. After all, what kind of woman slept with a man she'd known for less than a day? A stupid one, that's what kind. She waited for Dot to tell her so in no uncertain terms.

"Well, break out the champagne," Dot said. "It's about time."

Andie shot her a disgruntled look. "Have you been talking to my sister?"

"No. Why?"

"Nothing." Andie shook her head. "Nothing." She looked down, fiddling with the makeshift bandage around her hand, tucking the loose ends in to hold it secure. "I was counting on you to tell me what a fool I've been."

"Were you foolish?"

"Wasn't I?"

"Did he use protection?"

"Yes, of course," Andie said, blushing.

"There's no 'of course' about it. Lots of men won't," Dot informed her. "Did you enjoy it?"

"That's none of—" Andie began indignantly, and then broke off with a sigh. "Yes, I enjoyed it," she admitted, her blush deepening. "It was..." there was only one word to describe it "...extraordinary."

"Are either of you breaking any vows to anyone else?"

"No."

"Hurting anyone?"

"No-o-o," Andie said slowly. "I guess not."

"Well, then, what's the problem?"

"I'm older than he is, for one thing."

"By what?" Dot's expression told her what she thought of that excuse. "A couple of years?"

"Well, I'm his boss."

"So?"

"So, it's unprofessional. It could interfere with the job."

"Not if you're discreet about it."

"I'm not looking for a permanent relationship."

"Maybe he isn't, either. Have you thought of that?"

Andie's expression made it clear that she had. "But doesn't that make the whole thing kind of...I don't know..." She lifted one shoulder in a little shrug. "Tawdry?"

"That's something you'll have to decide for yourself, I guess. But if you really want my opinion...?"

"I do."

"Go for it."

Andie sighed. "I was afraid you'd say that."

7

JIM SANDED the dried marble glue on the mantle and fumed, nursing a steadily growing feeling of righteous indignation. After the night they'd spent together, after the things they'd done to and for and with each other, after *she'd* seduced *him*, dammit, she had the nerve to act as if she could barely recall his name.

Oh, and Jim, I want you to repack all this tile.

As if he was just another employee!

He'd seen her naked. He'd held her in his arms and made her writhe and moan and plead. And she'd done the same to him.

How dare she act as if it had never happened!

He'd always been the one who defined the boundaries of a relationship. He set the limits and decided how fast and how far things would progress. He was used to being in control, used to being deferred to by the women he went out with. Spoiled, his sisters would say, by the less-than-discriminating women he usually dated. He liked to think it worked both ways, that he gave as much as he got, but maybe his sisters had a point. He usually went for women with fewer sharp edges than Andrea Wagner possessed. Fewer complications, certainly. And he liked being spoiled. Was that such a crime?

What he didn't like, however—what he would *not* stand for—was being brushed off as if his very presence was an inconvenient reminder of a less-than-savory sexual encounter. There hadn't been anything unsavory about it at all, dammit!

So, okay, it had happened kind of fast. And maybe he hadn't been quite as up-front as he should have been about some things. But those things were relatively unimportant and could be cleared up later, after he'd done the job he'd been hired to do. What was important was that last night had been a uniquely satisfying experience—for *both* of them, he was sure—and fulfilling in a way that sex had never been for him before.

And he'd be damned if he'd let her turn it into a cheap one-night stand!

He crumbled the sandpaper he'd been using into a tight wad and with a muttered oath threw it at the wall, then turned toward the door, determined to find her and have it out. She could run, but she couldn't hide. At least, not for long.

She forestalled him by stepping into the room before he'd taken more than two steps away from the mantel.

"Could I talk to you?" she asked softly, giving him a hesitant little smile.

Some of the indignation went out of him at the sight of her, and he was nearly overwhelmed by the sudden need to cross the room and take her in his arms. Injured male pride kept him where he was. "You're the boss," he said with a negligent lift of one shoulder. "Talk."

Andie bit her lip. "You're mad at me. I guess I deserve that after the way I acted. I'm sorry," she said simply, offering reparation in the only way she knew how. "I didn't mean to hurt your feelings."

"You didn't hurt my feelings," he said quickly, despite the uncomfortable suspicion that she actually had.

Under the indignation and bruised male ego was a tender something that could conceivably have been labeled hurt feelings. It was another first for him. "You were right the first time," he said, putting it aside until he'd had more time to think about it. "You made me mad."

"And I'm sorry. Really." She crossed the room to stand in front of him. "I'd like to start over."

He cocked an eyebrow at her. "Over from where?"

"From this morning. My behavior was...regrettable and I'm ashamed of the way I acted."

"And last night?"

"Last night?"

"Was your behavior last night regrettable?" His voice was coolly dispassionate, as if he didn't really care what the answer was. "Are you ashamed of that, too?"

She frowned, considering his question.

He all but held his breath, waiting for her answer.

"I guess I should be, shouldn't I?" she said, and that small tender spot inside him began to throb painfully. "But—" she shook her head "—I'm not. Last night was wonderful. I don't regret a single minute of it."

The painful throb started to fade at her admission. But his bruised ego remained, demanding further penance before it would be soothed. "Then why the brush-off?"

"Stupidity," Andie said, more than willing to make amends in whatever way he required. "Uncertainty. I've never, uh...I've never slept with someone who works for me before. I didn't know how to handle it." She looked up at him appealingly. "I still don't."

That had Jim unbending, just a little. She looked so

sweet and sheepish and serious. "I've never slept with someone I work for before, either," he admitted.

"So **am** I forgiven for the way I acted?"

He unbent all the way. How could he not, with her standing there looking up at him with her big blue eyes all guileless and sincere, close enough so that her perfume tickled his nose and stirred his libido? "You're forgiven," he said, and put his hands on her arms, bending his head to hers.

"No." She put a hand to his chest, stopping him. "Not here."

Male ego reared its head again. "Why not here?" he demanded, suspicious and annoyed.

"Someone might see us," she said sharply, as if he should have known without being told.

That hurt. He felt it this time, no mistake, and acknowledged it for what it was. He took his hands off her and stepped back. "I thought you weren't ashamed."

"I'm not. " She took a step forward, closing the gap he had created by his retreat. "But this is a place of business. *My* business. I'm the boss and, as such, I have to maintain a position of authority. That's hard enough for a woman in the normal run of things, especially in construction. Can you imagine what would happen if someone walked in here and caught me kissing one of my employees?"

"I thought I was more than an employee."

"Not here, you're not," she retorted before she'd thought how it would sound to him. "Oh, don't look at me like that," she said when he scowled at her. "You know what I'm trying to say, even if I'm not saying it right."

In fact, Jim *did* know what she was trying to say. But that didn't mean he had to like it. He stuck his hands in his front pockets and hunched his shoulders, giving her a look any mother of a two-year-old would recognize.

"Business is business," she said earnestly, and took another step forward, inadvertently backing him up against the fireplace in her single-minded effort to make him understand her point of view. "And pleasure is pleasure and a smart woman—a smart *person*—doesn't mix the two."

Suddenly, Jim began to feel like Doris Day again, in the inevitable scene in every movie where Rock Hudson backs her against his desk or a wall or the door of a limousine. It wasn't exactly the same, since Rock had usually been bent on seduction, and seduction was the furthest thing from Andie's mind at the moment. But it tickled Jim's funny bone just the same, and his sense of the ridiculous took over. He felt like he should be defending his virtue.

Andie reached out and laid her hand on his chest again, in supplication and entreaty this time, rather than refusal. "If you'd just think about it a minute, you'd realize that I'm... What?" she demanded, seeing the faint hint of something in his eyes.

"Does this mean you're just using me for sex?" he asked, straight-faced only because he was biting the inside of his cheek to keep from grinning. "Your boy toy on the side?"

"No, of course not!" she denied vehemently, although, semantics aside, that was exactly what she was hoping to do. What else would you call it? She didn't intend for whatever was between them to develop into anything permanent. "What I feel for you is much more complicated than that. I want us to, uh...date."

"Well, that's one word for it."

She shot him a fulminating glare. "I would simply prefer that our relationship not become a source of gossip on the job site, that's all," she said primly, struggling to hold on to her temper. The man was deliberately misunderstanding her. "I should think you'd prefer—"

That look in his eyes deepened, becoming recognizable as a gleam of unholy amusement. Her eyes narrowed. "What's so funny?"

"You're so cute when you're being earnest."

She stared up at him for a minute, stupefied by his reaction to her impassioned apology. What had happened to the hurt feelings and the bruised ego? The injured pride in need of soothing?

"This is all just a big joke to you, isn't it? You haven't heard a word I've said." She thumped her hand against his chest, using the momentum to push herself away from him. "Well, fine. Forget it. I've changed my mind. I don't—"

He reached out and grabbed her wrist, keeping her from turning away. "Andrea, sweetheart, I was listening to every word. Honest. And I agree with you. I just—"

"Don't you sweetheart me, you big jerk." She tried to tug her wrist from his grasp. "Let go."

"What happened to your hand?"

"My hand?" Andie had to look at it before she remembered she'd done anything to it at all. "It's nothing. Just a scratch." She tugged at her hand again. "Now let go."

"There's too much blood on that bandanna for it to be

just a scratch. No, dammit, hold still and let me look at it. You can hit me after."

"I wasn't going to hit you," she said, as he reached up with his free hand to unwind the bandanna from around her knuckles. "Unlike some people—" she tilted her head back, looking down her nose at him "—I don't depend on brute strength to get my way. I...oh." She winced and sucked in her breath.

"It's stuck to the wound," he told her unnecessarily. "It's going to have to be soaked off."

"Oh, for heaven's sake. Just yank it off." She closed her eyes. "Go ahead. I can take it."

"Well, I can't."

Andie opened her eyes. "Wuss," she said, and reached up with her free hand, ripping it free before he could move to stop her. Yelping as fresh blood welled, she pressed the bloodstained bandanna against the jagged scratch with little daubing motions, staunching the flow.

"Jeez, give me that." Jim plucked the bandanna from her fingers and stuffed it into his tool belt. "It's filthy. Here." He pulled a clean handkerchief out of his back pocket and pressed it to the wound. "Where's the first-aid kit?"

"I don't need first aid," Andie objected. "It's just a scratch. It'll stop bleeding in a minute."

"Scratches get infected."

"This one won't. I had a tetanus booster last year."

"The first-aid kit?" he repeated.

"There's one in my tool box," she said, recognizing an immovable object when she saw one. "It's in the master bathroom."

Keeping her hand in his, with his handkerchief

pressed to the scratch, he led her into the bathroom. "Sit," he ordered, pushing her down onto the closed mahogany lid of the painted porcelain toilet. "Hold that right there." He positioned her fingers over the handkerchief, then turned to open her tool box.

It was really quite sweet the way he fussed over her, Andie thought, watching him search through her huge red tool box for the first-aid kit. He was arrogant and overbearing and as cocky as a rooster but...sweet. She hadn't been fussed over by a man in...well, she hadn't been fussed over by a man since she'd left her father's house.

Nathan Bishop was a born fussbudget who was always trying to take care of things for his womenfolk, whether they wanted things taken care of or not. Andie's ex-husband, on the other hand, had expected *her* to fuss over *him*. That's what wives were for, after all. Andie had done her best to be a good wife for far longer than she should have, and she was determined never to repeat the mistake. She would be no man's wife, ever again.

"GIVE ME YOUR HAND," Jim said as he went down on one knee in front of her. The first-aid kit was open on the floor beside him.

Andie gave him her hand.

He lifted the blood-spattered handkerchief. "It looks like it's stopped bleeding."

"I told you."

He ignored that and tore open a presoaked, antiseptic pad. "This might sting a little," he warned as he pressed it to the wound.

It did sting—more than a little—but Andie sucked in

her breath and let him have his way. He cleaned the jagged scratch gently, then leaned forward to blow on it and take some of the sting away.

"Where'd you learn to do that?"

"My sister Janet has four kids. Jessie's got one, too. You pick things up." He cleaned his own fingers with the pad, then squeezed out a dab of antiseptic cream and daubed it all along the scratch, which was long, but not deep, running across the back of her hand, just under her knuckles. The wound was already beginning to scab over, but Jim decided it needed a bandage, anyway. "To keep it clean and protect it from opening up again," he said as he made a dressing of neatly folded gauze and two narrow strips of adhesive tape.

Andie thought it was overkill, but she didn't have the heart to tell him. "Thank you," she said, because what else could she say?

"You're welcome." Jim bent his head then and kissed her knuckles, just above the dressing. "There. All better now," he said in a soft singsong cadence, as if he were soothing a young niece or nephew.

And, unaccountably, Andie felt tears sting her eyes. He was so darn sweet. Why did he have to be so sweet? She blinked and reached out, touching his cheek with her fingertips. "I really didn't mean to hurt your feelings," she said, when he looked up in silent inquiry.

"I know." He lifted his hand to the back of hers, pressing it to his cheek for a moment before he drew it down to his lips to place a soft kiss in the callused little palm. "And I didn't mean to laugh at you. I *wasn't* laughing at you, really, so much as I was laughing at us and how silly we were being." He drew her hands together on her lap, holding them comfortably in both of his as he knelt there on one knee in front of her. "I understood what you were saying. And I agree. Carrying on at the office, so to speak, is never a good idea." He gave her a wicked smile, reflected in his eyes. "So we'll carry on everywhere else. Okay?"

Andie couldn't help but smile back. "Okay," she agreed, wishing he'd ignore her strictures about proper behavior on the job site and kiss her senseless, the way he had last night.

Jim read the invitation in her eyes, and his own gaze deepened and heated, intensifying the golden shards in his brandy-colored eyes. He leaned forward, just slightly, and waited. She leaned forward slowly, making them both wonder if she'd give in to the temptation he offered.

"Excuse me. Andie?"

Andie jerked bolt upright. She would have jumped up and started babbling excuses and explanations, but Jim clasped her hands more tightly, pressing down on her knees, and held her where she was, giving her the seconds she needed to think. She took a quick breath and turned her head toward the door. "Yes, Booker?" she said calmly. "What is it?"

"You told me to come down here when I was finished in the servants' bathroom." Booker's face was flushed and the tips of his ears were bright red. His gaze darted back and forth between his boss and the man kneeling at her feet. "And I'm, uh, finished."

"Oh, good. That's good. Then we can get started." She turned back to Jim. "Are we all set here?"

"As long as you keep the bandage on and the dirt out, it should be fine." He clicked the first-aid kit shut as he spoke, then picked it up and rose to his feet, stepping back so Andie could stand up.

Rising, she glanced at her watch, turning her wrist so the bandage on the back of her hand was clearly visible to her young apprentice. "It's a quarter to twelve," she said, as if her words were meant for both of them equally. "We'd just about get started in here and it would be time to stop for lunch. So why don't we knock off now, even though it's a few minutes early, and I'll see you—" she smiled at Booker "—back here at one o'clock, on the dot. We'll start with the mahogany surround and the vanity cabinet."

"We could get started now, if you want," Booker said earnestly, casting a quick, suspicious glance at Jim. "I don't mind taking my lunch break later."

Jim raised an eyebrow, countering the younger man's look with a bland smile.

"*I'd* mind if you took it later," Andie said, unaware of the byplay between her two apprentices. "Can't have my employees keeling over from hunger. The union frowns on that sort of thing."

"Well...okay. If you're sure." Booker shot another glare at Jim. "I'll be back as quick as I can."

"One o'clock will be fine," she called after him, then waited until she heard his size-twelve work boots pounding down the stairs. She turned to Jim. "Do you think he bought it?"

"Oh, I think so. As far as he's concerned you're an innocent little lamb who has no idea she's being stalked by the big bad wolf. The kid's gonzo over you," he added when she just stood there, looking at him.

"Gonzo?" It took her a minute. "You mean he's got a

crush on... Oh, no. That's crazy. He's just shy around women."

Jim snorted. "If that were true Tiffany would have scared him off by now."

"Well...maybe," she agreed. Tiffany had been known to make grown men tremble in fear with her man-eater routine, but Booker didn't seem to have any trouble dealing with her. "I'm his boss," Andie said. "Naturally, he's a little intimidated."

"Sweetheart, the kid's infatuated, not intimidated. If looks could kill, I'd be stretched out on the floor right now, deader than a mackerel in the frozen-food section."

"But that's ridiculous. He can't be more than a couple of years older than Kyle."

"And we both know Kyle isn't interested in girls yet, don't we?" he said, not so subtly reminding her of the stash of condoms in her son's dresser drawer.

Andie flushed, remembering how many of them they'd borrowed. "That's not what I meant," she said primly, refusing to concede the point. "What I meant was, I'm almost old enough to be his mother. Boys Booker's age don't get crushes on women my age."

"Why not?" Jim's lips quirked up at one corner in a little, self-mocking smile. "I did."

8

"WELL, WELL, WELL," Tiffany's words were accompanied by a sly, teasing grin. "'It looks like Booker wasn't so far off the mark, after all."

Andie gave the younger woman a wary look from under her lashes as she took a seat on one of the wooden benches in the gazebo. "Off the mark about what?" She snapped open the latches on her vintage Bugs Bunny lunch box as she asked the question, trying to appear casual and only mildly interested.

"He said sweet ch— Oww!" Tiffany shot a reproachful look at Dot as she reached down to rub her shin. "What was that for?"

Dot frowned. "His name's Jim, remember?"

"Oh, right. Sorry. I forgot we weren't supposed to call him sw—uh, that." She turned back to Andie. "Booker said he caught Jim coming on to you upstairs in the master bathroom. Is that true?"

Dot snorted. "Good Lord, girl, you're as nosy as a census taker. Did you ever stop to think Andie's personal life might be none of your business?"

"It's all right," Andie said. "It isn't personal. Booker just misunderstood what he saw. Jim was bandaging my hand." She held out the appendage in question. "I had a little accident."

"And the hickey on your neck? Was that an accident, too?"

Andie slapped her hand over the mark on her neck.

Dot threw up her hands. "Tiffany, for heaven's sake!"

"What? I tell you guys all about my sex life, don't I? It's only fair you share some of the juicy details of yours once in a while."

"Did it ever occur to you that we might not be interested in your sex life?" Dot asked.

"No." Tiffany's expression clearly said the thought had never occurred to her. "Everybody's interested in sex, whether they'll admit it or not. So—" she slanted an eager, sideways look at Andie "—is he as good as he looks?"

Andie sighed. She'd been involved in an intimate relationship for one day—less than one day!—and it was already a hot topic of discussion on the job site.

"Does that mean yes?" Tiffany persisted, all but licking her lips in anticipation of the answer.

Andie had to laugh. She must have been crazy to think she could keep her relationship with Jim a secret. The only thing left to do was brazen it out. Besides, she wasn't ashamed. She'd only wanted to avoid gossip and speculation. Which, obviously, hadn't worked, or she wouldn't be sitting there, trying to dodge questions about her sex life.

"Yes." She smiled, remembering. "That means he's as good as he looks."

"I knew it!" Tiffany crowed. "So spill."

"Tiffany, for heaven's sake. Show a little decorum. Not everybody likes to brag about their sex life. Besides—" Dot tilted her head sideways, toward the low brick wall a few yards away where Booker sat with Matthew and some of the younger members of the stonemason's crew "—this is hardly the place to talk about it."

Tiffany scooted closer to Andie on the bench seat and leaned in close. "Give us all the details," she said, her voice low. "And don't leave anything out."

For just a moment, Andie was tempted. It had been so wonderful, so special, so unexpected, that she longed to share it. She longed to hold it up to the light of day and show it off like a precious jewel. She wanted to talk about what he'd done, what he'd said, how he'd made her feel, what it all meant. She wanted to examine the nuances of emotion and sensation with an understanding, receptive audience. She wanted to brag. She shook her head, resisting the temptation. "It's personal."

"Well, of course it's personal. That's the point. We're all friends here." Tiffany put her hand on Andie's knee and squeezed encouragingly. "Feel free to spill your guts."

Andie reached into her lunch box, pulled out a sandwich and began unwrapping it. "Why don't you tell me what happened at Varga's last night, instead? From what you said earlier, it sounds like you had a good time."

"Not as good as you had, I bet," Tiffany groused.

Andie's smile was impish. "Probably not," she agreed, and sank her teeth into her tuna fish on whole wheat.

"IT HAD TO HAVE HAPPENED during the lunch break—" Mary wrung her hands as she spoke "—because it was all right when I left. At least, I think it was all right."

"Yes, of course it was all right," Tiffany said, and for once there was nothing teasing or flirtatious in her manner. "We took it out of the crate this morning and I checked it over myself, prism by prism, to make sure it was all there. We were going to hang it before lunch but it took longer to install the electrical box than I thought it would." Tiffany turned to Andie. "And then Booker came and told us you'd said we could take lunch a little early. That worked out great for Mary, since this is the day she always takes her daughter for her allergy shot. We set the chandelier in the corner there, where it would be out of the way until after lunch."

"And when I came back—" Mary gestured at the chandelier that lay on its side, so many of its delicate crystal prisms broken "—it was like that."

"It could have been an accident," Andie said, wanting very much to believe that. "It could have just fallen over. Or someone could have accidentally knocked it over and they're afraid to say so. But they don't have to be. I wouldn't hold it ag—"

"This was no accident." Knees spread, elbows on his splayed thighs, Jim was crouched down next to the broken chandelier, examining the damage. "Some of these prisms aren't just broken, they've been shattered and ground to a powder under someone's boot."

"Someone's boot?" Andie put a hand on his shoulder and leaned over, peering down onto the floor between his knees. "How can you tell?"

"Here." He pointed, his finger hovering over the site without touching it. "And here. You can just see the imprint of a heel. Of course—" he looked up at the people surrounding them "—it's not going to do much good as evidence, since you've all been stomping all over, contaminating the crime scene."

Everyone took a quick step or two back, away from

the broken chandelier. A few of them lifted their feet to check the soles of their shoes for fragments of glass. Some of them, including Andie, found what they were looking for.

"It's highly unlikely the police will be able to get anything useful from this mess," Jim said as he rose. "But let's everyone back off, anyway, in case there's some evidence you haven't already destroyed."

"The police?" Andie's eyes went wide. "I'm not calling the police."

"Why the hell not?"

"What good would it do? You said yourself we've probably destroyed any evidence there might have been."

"You still need to report it. Get some pictures taken of those." He waved an impatient hand at the shoe prints on the floor. "Dust for fingerprints in case the perp touched anything. You don't know what will turn up until you look."

"I don't agree," Andie said. "There isn't any evidence that this is anything more than an accident, despite that footprint. As you said, it could have been made by any one of us in the last few minutes."

"We both know it wasn't."

Andie ignored that. "So what have we got here, really? A broken chandelier, that's it. What crime would I report? Breaking and entering?" She shook her head. "The doors are unlocked. Some of them are even standing wide-open. And criminal trespass wasn't committed, either, since the house isn't posted as private property." She hadn't been a policeman's daughter all her life without learning the rudiments of the laws her father enforced. "Technically, no crime was committed here."

"Everything you say is absolutely true," Jim agreed, "and if this were an isolated incident, I'd agree with you about not involving the police. But everyone here knows it isn't an isolated incident, not by a long shot."

"Jim's right." Dot put in her two cents worth. "You should report it."

"No. I can handle it myself. I *will* handle it myself." Andie took a deep breath to get herself under control, then turned toward the employees who stood behind her in a silent semicircle. "We're instituting some new procedures around here, as of this minute. From now on, the outside doors are to be kept closed and locked unless one of the crew is working where he or she can monitor who goes in or out. The same goes for the windows on the ground floor. You leave the room, you close the window. You lock it. No exceptions."

"You do that, it's gonna get mighty hot in here," Pete said.

"I'll get some fans. Tiffany, Mary, I want you two to clean up all this glass before somebody gets hurt, and then I want you to get the chandelier hung. Count up how many prisms were broken and let me know so I can order replacements. Booker, you go on upstairs and get to work on the mahogany surround on that tub. If you have any questions, ask Dot. The rest of you get busy with whatever you were scheduled to do this afternoon." When they hesitated, she waved them away with both hands. "Go on. I'm not paying you to stand around and gape like a bunch of spectators at a car accident."

"And what are you going to do?" Jim asked.

Andie turned around to face him. "I'm going to the hardware store for a couple of fans and some heavy-duty locks."

"And you think that will take care of the problem?"

"I think it's a step in the right direction."

"Reporting this to the police would be a better step."

She gave him a level look. "You said you wouldn't offer me any more advice unless I asked for it, remember?"

"I said I'd *try* not to."

"Try harder," she snapped, and moved to go around him.

He put out a hand and stopped her. "Just what have you got against cops? Your father was a cop, for crying out loud."

"Exactly," she said, and shook off his hand.

THERE WERE TWO MESSAGES on the answering machine when Andie got home that night. The first was from her daughter. The second was from the heavy breather.

She hit the Stop button as soon as she realized it wasn't a legitimate call, intending to erase it as she'd done with all the others, but then she paused and hit Rewind to listen again. It was a man, she was sure of that, even though he was trying to disguise his voice by whispering. His words weren't really obscene, just oddly disturbing in a way she couldn't quite describe. "I want to take care of you," he whispered. "Let me take care of you."

"Not a chance, pal," Andie said aloud, and stabbed the Erase button with her index finger.

The phone began to ring as the tape rewound.

Startled, Andie drew her hand back and stared at the ringing phone.

He'd never called in the evening before; he'd always called during the day when she wasn't home.

She grabbed the receiver. "Listen, buster—"

"Mom?"

"Oh, Emily, darling. It's you." Andie pressed her hand to her wildly pounding heart. "I was just getting ready to return your call. How are you, sweetheart?"

Emily launched into an impassioned tirade against her bossy older brother and the unreasonable grandfather who insisted on treating her like a child. She'd been on the phone about a half an hour, having exhausted their male relatives as a topic and gone on to the cute boy who worked at the marina, when Andie heard the unmistakable sound of a Harley-Davidson rumbling in the distance. She cocked her head, listening for Jim with one ear, trying to catch what her daughter was saying with the other.

"Um-hmm. Green eyes on a boy are very cool." Andie stretched the telephone cord as far as it would go and reached out with her free hand, flicking up the edge of the bedroom curtain. She could see a motorcycle coming down the street, too far away to tell if the helmeted rider was who she hoped it was. But her heart skipped a beat anyway.

"Yes, I know boys can be very con..."

The motorcycle slowed and turned into her driveway.

Andie's heart jumped into her throat.

It was Jim.

He was here!

After what had happened this afternoon, she'd figured he would never show up tonight. And she hadn't changed or showered or—

"Chris caught you kissing who?" She dropped the curtain and focused all her attention on what her daughter was telling her. "Oh." She put a hand to her heart, forgetting why it had started beating double time in the first place. "Oh, he caught you *practicing* kissing. With who? On your hand?" *Thank you, God!* "No, Emily, you're not a perverted sicko freak. Your brother doesn't know what he's talking about. Well, yes, your friend Jennifer is right. Partly right, anyway. Kissing can be very nice. If you're kissing the right—"

The doorbell chimed, three melodious notes that vibrated through the air. Andie barely registered the sound.

"—person. But twelve is too young to be kissing a boy for real. Oh, Jennifer's thirteen. I see. Well, that's still too young, to my way of thinking. How old is old enough depends on a lot of things, honey. How mature the girl is, how long she's known the boy. Lots of—"

The doorbell rang again. Andie continued to ignore it. She was completely focused on giving advice to her daughter.

"—different things. Kissing isn't something you should rush into without giving it a lot of thought." *Lots and lots of thought. Years of thought!* "Kissing is serious business and— Fishing? But what about... Yes. Yes, of course. All right, you go fishing with Grandpa, darling. I know how impatient he can be. But promise me one thing before you hang up, okay? Promise me you'll stick to just *practicing* kissing, at least for the rest of this week, and we'll talk more about it when I come up this weekend. Yes, I will. Your yellow sundress with the bows on the shoulders. Yes, I know which one you mean. Okay. I love you, too, darling." Her "goodbye" was spoken to empty air.

She cradled the receiver gently, her expression wistful and a little apprehensive. Her little girl was growing up so fast. Last week Emily's conversation had been all about the neat new outfit she wanted for Barbie. This week it was kissing. Andie was almost afraid to wonder what next week would bring.

The doorbell rang again, the three notes sounding strident this time, and impatient, and Andie suddenly recalled exactly who was outside on her front porch, waiting to be let in. She ran out of her bedroom and down the stairs, her work boots clunking on the steps; she was as nervous as a schoolgirl afraid her beau would change his mind and leave before she could get the door open.

He was standing on the porch with a pizza box in one hand and a bottle of red wine in the other, his index finger extended out from the neck of the bottle as he prepared to press the doorbell again. He'd showered and shaved and was wearing a clean white polo shirt, faded jeans and a battered, brown-leather bomber jacket that made him look like one of those hunky guys in a blue-jeans commercial.

Andie sighed and laid her cheek on her hand where it rested on the edge of the door. "Hi," she said, and smiled at him through the fine mesh of the screen.

"Hi, yourself." His answering smile made her toes curl inside her work boots. "You took so long I was beginning to think you were still mad at me."

Andie blinked in surprise. "Why would I be mad at you?"

He cocked an eyebrow. "You gave a pretty good imitation of mad this afternoon."

"It was the situation, not you."

"Well, in that case, how about letting me in before the pizza gets stone-cold?"

"Oh, yes. Of course. Come in." She pushed the screen open and stepped back, catching a whiff of pepperoni and aftershave as he crossed in front of her. The fresh citrusy scent reminded her that she was still wearing the same clothes she'd had on all day. She suddenly felt like a grubby little worm next to all his glorious masculine pulchritude.

"Why don't we take that pizza into the kitchen?" She reached for the box and headed on down the hall toward the back of the house, trusting that he would follow. "We'll stick it in the oven for a few minutes to reheat." After sliding it into the oven, box and all, she turned the dial to Warm and then yanked open a drawer. "Here's the corkscrew."

He caught her hand in his. "You took off the bandage."

"It got kind of grimy and kept catching on things."

"It doesn't look any the worse for wear, I guess. No redness." He rubbed his thumb lightly across the length of the scabbed-over scratch. "Does that hurt at all?"

"No." Andie eased her hand—her grubby, callused hand—out of his and reached to open a cupboard. "Wineglasses," she said, as if he might not know what they were. She took them out of the cabinet, carefully, by their stems, and set them on the counter next to the bottle of wine. "You go ahead and open it. Pour yourself a glass and take it out on the back porch, if you like. It's nice out there this time of day. I'm going to run upstairs and take a quick shower." She ran a hand through her hair, setting it all on end. "I would have done it already, but there were some, uh, messages on the answering machine and then Emily called and, well..." She shrugged. "I didn't really think we were still on for tonight."

"Why would you think that? I said I'd bring dinner."

"I thought *you* might be mad at *me*," she admitted.

"The situation," he said, repeating her words back to her. "Not you."

"We argued. I yelled at you."

"Yeah? So?"

So, her ex-husband had always used her infrequent bursts of temper against her, retreating into disapproving silence until she apologized for whatever ill, real or imagined, she had done him. It had been one of his primary methods of control, and she had hated it and him and herself because it had worked so well. On some level she had been prepared to encounter, and resist, the same treatment from Jim, and was disconcerted to find it wasn't necessary.

"I'll go take that shower now."

Jim reached out, moved by a look in her eyes that he couldn't quite define, and curled his hand around her nape. "In a minute," he murmured, and bent his head to hers.

Andie stiffened in surprise. "I'll get you all dir—"

The kiss was deep and rich and leisurely, and by the time he lifted his lips from hers, she was as boneless and pliant as a rag doll.

"Mmm. Nice." He tilted his head, touching his forehead to hers. "I've been wanting to do that all day."

"And I've been wanting you to do it all day."

"Have you? You hid it pretty well."

She smiled. "Except for this morning when Booker walked in on us. I wasn't hiding it then."

"Ah, well." He pressed another soft kiss on her mouth. "You were injured. Your resistance was down."

"It seems as if my resistance is always down around you."

"Oh, yeah? Then how about I come up and wash your back for you? See if I can lower it a little more?"

She pulled away from him then, reluctantly. "Dinner first. Otherwise, I won't have the strength for whatever it is you've got in mind once you've got my resistance lowered."

"You won't need strength," he growled, and drew her in for yet another kiss.

She acquiesced for a long, delicious moment, reveling in the white-hot attraction that zinged back and forth between them, delighting in the way he held her, so gently yet so firmly, with nothing but his hand at the back of her head and the heat of his mouth on hers. He didn't push or hurry or harry her. He didn't grab or demand. He tasted and savored, letting the anticipation—and her response—swell and build in its own time, to its own internal rhythm.

"I'll hurry," she whispered, and slipped from his grasp.

She raced through her shower, slowing down only to run a razor over her legs and underarms, speeding up again when she slathered on scented body lotion and spritzed herself with cologne. Her hair, thank goodness, took only a brisk rubbing with a towel to dry and a quick finger-combing to style. Her makeup was minimal—a little mascara, a dusting of blusher, a dab of clear lip gloss. And then she paused in front of her closet, standing there in her flower-sprigged bikini panties and matching baby T-shirt, her hand on a long, pastel-blue dress, aghast at the mindlessness of what she was doing.

She'd always done the total woman routine for Kevin, bathing and changing from the skin out every day before he came home from work, so she'd be sweet and fresh and feminine for him. He hadn't liked her grubby from the garden, or sweaty from housework, or frazzled from dealing with the children. He'd liked the house clean, the kids quiet, dinner ready to put on the table and her at the front door with a Scotch and soda in her hand. It had been easier to go along with him, easier than dealing with the injured silences and pointed barbs when she tried to assert herself.

And she had been following the same pattern with Jim. Oh, not at work. On the job, she knew who she was. She didn't have any preconceived, ingrained notions of what was expected of her or how she was supposed to behave at work. But get her back on familiar turf, in a woman's place, as it were, and she reverted to type. She turned into the same spineless, mindlessly accommodating wimp Kevin had always insisted was a woman's true lot in life; she turned into a *wife*.

Except that Jim hadn't insisted on or expected anything.

He found her sexy in overalls and work boots, and proved it, too, by kissing her senseless while she was still covered with the day's grime. He didn't carry a grudge because she'd yelled at him, nor did he upbraid her for the unfeminine behavior she'd exhibited in asserting herself. He hadn't tried to punish her with silence, or force her to play guessing games about what she'd done wrong, for the simple reason that he didn't think she'd done anything wrong. *She* was the one who was ascribing motives and jumping to unwarranted conclusions. *He* hadn't made a single gender-based assumption.

So if she made herself up and put on a dress now, it was because she *wanted* to put it on, not because some man expected her to do it. Far from expecting it, the man waiting in her kitchen would probably be surprised to see her come floating down the stairs in more feminine attire. She grinned at herself in the mirror and decided to give him an even bigger surprise.

She shimmied out of her panties and the form-fitting little T-shirt, tossing them behind her onto the bed before she reached for the loose cotton dress she'd intended to wear over them. It went on over bare skin instead. The wide straps sat lightly on her shoulders; the soft, well-washed fabric just grazed her breasts and hips; the hem fluttered modestly at midcalf. She was completely, even demurely covered. And she felt completely, deliciously, wickedly decadent.

More than a match for the gorgeous, sensual man waiting for her downstairs.

She flicked her fingers through her wispy bangs, tightened the pearl stud in one earlobe and, humming softly under her breath, headed toward the kitchen, her bare feet soundless on the carpeted stairs and the smooth hardwood floor of the hallway. Maybe she'd flash him halfway through dinner á la Sharon Stone in *Basic Instinct*. Or maybe she'd stand up to pour him a second glass of wine and lean over just a bit too far, innocently exposing her all. He'd be able to see bare skin down to her toes if she did that. And she'd end up in his lap, or on the table, or against the wall. She quickened her pace, following her nose from the kitchen to the seldom-used dining room.

Jim hadn't sat idly by while she showered and changed. He'd found dishes and cutlery, placemats and napkins, and arranged them on the dining-room table. He'd put the pizza on a tray and poured the wine and put on some music, filling the house with hot, seductive sounds of Stevie Ray Vaughn on guitar. He'd unearthed a trio of fat ivory candles from the depths of her china cabinet and lit them, even though it wasn't quite twilight. And now he was drawing the drapes over the wide picture window, shutting the world out, closing them in....

The expression on his face when he turned and saw her standing in the doorway was worth any twinge of anxiety she'd felt about wearing a dress. His eyes widened in appreciation, his body tensed and tightened, his nostrils flared ever so slightly—a male animal scenting his mate. The anticipation thrumming so pleasantly through Andie's body turned into a torrent of tempestuous, insistent, blood-boiling need in an instant. It suddenly felt as if she was wearing far too many clothes.

Without a word, she reached up and pushed the straps of her sundress from her shoulders, letting the weight and volume of the fabric pull it down her body. And when she was naked, she stood there motionless, like a modern version of Botticelli's *Venus*, with her dress pooled around her feet like pale blue sea foam. She made no effort to hide herself from his eyes. There was no teasing placement of her hands on her body, no demurely bent knee, no crossed arms. It was a simple, straightforward statement of her need, an offering of self without coyness or pretense.

Jim nearly swallowed his tongue. Like a fish out of water, gasping for air, he opened his mouth to speak, then closed it again. He could hear his blood pounding in his ears, feel it racing through his veins, feel it tightening and swelling every cell in his body. There was only one answer for such honesty.

As silently as she had disrobed for him, he disrobed for her. He sat on the smooth wooden chair at the head of the table and unlaced his heavy black boots, dropping them and his socks on the floor. He peeled off his shirt next, and then his jeans and briefs so that he stood before her, Adam to her Eve, as naked and vulnerable as she was.

They stared at each other for an unending moment, drinking in the beauty of each other's physical form, visually caressing the angles and curves of each other's body. Andie could feel the scorching heat of his gaze like a lover's touch as it drifted over her breasts and belly and lingered to probe the feminine mysteries hidden beneath the pale thatch of hair between her thighs. He could feel the warmth of her thoughts as she mentally stroked his shoulders and chest and the hard, throbbing flesh between his legs.

She trembled.

He trembled, too.

And still they looked, absorbing each other through sight alone until, finally, looking was no longer enough and they moved toward each other, driven by the need to touch what was so greatly desired. Palm-to-palm first; small, delicate hands measured against larger, darker ones. Callused fingertips skimming delicately over slanted cheekbones and the hard curve of a jaw, down a slender throat, over bulging biceps and shoulders, molding the sloping curve of a waist, tracing the hard planes of a flat stomach, caressing the smooth, enticing swell of hip and thigh. Chest-to-breast, then, just brushing, ever so lightly, sending ripples of sensation dancing over receptive nerve endings. Lips touching, tasting, retreating, only to return and taste again. Loin-to-loin, lightly, a mere glancing touch to tease and excite and arouse.

And then, suddenly, two bodies pressed tightly together. Eager and hot and greedy. Arms hard and clinging. Hands frantic, kneading and stroking. Mouths open and seeking. Lips and teeth and tongues nibbling and nipping, sucking, licking. Hips grinding, slowly, savagely, hard to soft, male to female, each needing desperately to be part of the other.

Jim slid his hands to the backs of her thighs, lifting her, urging her to open and accept him. Andie spread her legs willingly, eagerly, wrapping them around his waist, and took him inside her.

"Yes! Oh, yes."

They sighed in satisfaction and desire, and began straining for the necessary friction that would give them what they needed.

"More."

Jim sank to his knees with Andie locked tightly in his arms, and then leaned forward, putting one hand out to brace them as he laid her on her back, half on, half off of the patterned Turkish carpet beneath the table. She could feel the smooth hardwood floor beneath her bare bottom and the softness of the carpet beneath her back and Jim on top of her, his body hard and straining and strong, filling her...filling the emptiness...filling her whole world.

He began to move, pumping slowly, so excruciatingly slowly, in and out, thrusting powerfully, deeply into her, withdrawing to the point where she thought she would die if he withdrew any further.

She began to writhe, her body lifting into his, her hips rolling up to meet each powerful thrust of his pelvis.

But it wasn't enough.

Not hard enough.

Not deep enough.

Not fast enough.

Not...nearly...enough.

She reached up and behind her, grasping at the table leg with both hands to anchor herself against his great, surging thrusts, and planted her feet flat on the bare hardwood floor to give herself more leverage, pushing her hips up and into him.

He was braced on his hands above her, every muscle in his body bulging and tense, his eyes wide-open and locked on hers as he worked to give them both what they needed. Sweat broke out across his shoulders and chest, evidence of the rigid control he was exerting over both of them, but still he moved slowly, powerfully, letting the tension build, drawing her body tighter and tighter, pushing her higher and higher.

She began to pant, taking in great gulps of air. "Jim. Jim, please," she sobbed. "Please."

"Come to me," he crooned, as breathless, as tortured as she was. He moved up on her body, changing the angle slightly, a tiny, necessary fraction of an inch that uncreased the friction, and surged into her again, faster now, and harder. "Come to me, baby."

She came.

Gloriously.

In a wild, tempestuous rush of sensation that stretched every nerve ending in her body to its absolute limit and held it there forever before it snapped. She moaned, a long, low, tortured sound that ended in a triumphant scream as every muscle and sinew in her body celebrated the exquisite release of tension.

Jim's body followed hers over the precipice of sensation, tensing for a long, agonizing, deliciously savage moment before tumbling into blinding, mind-numbing, soul-shattering ecstasy. And then he shuddered and collapsed to lay, exhilarated and exhausted, in her arms, feeling as if every part of him had touched every part of her in that sublime moment. Body and soul. Mind and heart. Everything.

Sex had never been like that for him before. So intense. So consuming. So powerful and primitive and wonderful. So *necessary*. He could think of only one reason it would be that way now.

"Oh, God, Andrea." His voice grated in her ear, thick with spent passion, raw with the wonder of what he was feeling. "I've fallen in love with you."

9

ANDIE'S FIRST REACTION to his declaration was delight. "You're in love with me? Oh, Jim...I..." And then she panicked. He was in love with her! How could he be in love with her? She didn't want him to be in love with her! This wasn't about love; it was about sex, pure and simple. "Don't be ridiculous!"

"Ridiculous?" Jim mumbled the word into the warm curve of her neck as if he didn't quite understand its meaning. The blood hadn't made it all the way back to his brain yet, and his muscles were still quivering with exquisite release. He couldn't quite concentrate on anything except the glorious feelings flooding through him.

He'd never been in love before, he realized. Not really. Oh, there'd been that heady combination of lust, fondness and gratitude he'd felt for Patty Newcomb, the first girl he'd ever had sex with. And a similar feeling a few years later for the more experienced young woman who'd introduced him to the unparalleled joys of fellatio. And there was that time in his early twenties, right after college, when he'd confused a desire to move on to the next stage of his life with something stronger, and had almost gotten himself engaged. But it turned out he and his girlfriend wanted different things, and neither of them had cared enough to make the necessary sacrifices. The affair had died a juiceless, unlamented death.

Since then, he'd kept it light, waiting, playing the field, knowing that when he found the right woman, everything would just naturally fall into place.

And it had.

Except...

Except that the object of his newly discovered affections wasn't cooperating. He gathered his befuddled wits and his flagging energy and pushed himself up onto his elbows so he could frown at her.

"Just why in hell is my being in love with you ridiculous?"

"Because it is, that's why. Because I'm older than you and—"

"Six years," he scoffed. "Big deal."

"And I have kids. I have *three* kids, remember?"

"So? I like kids."

"And because...because..." Because men in love had expectations. They had needs and requirements. They made demands. And women in love had to meet those needs and accommodate those demands. "Because I didn't think you were looking for anything permanent, that's why."

"I didn't think I was, either, but I seem to have changed my mind."

"You can't change your mind now," she told him peevishly. "It's not fair."

"Not fair? What the hell does that mean? What's fairness got to do with it?"

"Nothing, obviously!" She put her hands on his shoulders and shoved. "Now get off of me. I'm hungry and the pizza's getting cold."

"Hungry!" He pushed himself up onto both hands. "I tell you I love you and all you have to say is you're *hungry?* No. No, wait." He reared back, rising to his knees between her splayed thighs, and scowled down at her. "You said I was ridiculous, too, didn't you? Ridiculous!" he fumed, indignant and incensed and insulted all at once. "Hell, if anyone's being ridiculous, it's you. Here we are, buck naked on your dining-room floor because we couldn't wait another second to get our hands on each other. Both of us are wrung out from the most incredible lovemaking I've ever—"

"Sex." She pushed herself backward, away from him, and sat up, nearly whacking her head on the edge of the table as she did so. "We had sex."

That hurt. A lot. "We made love, dammit! We..." Something in her eyes, some fleeting expression, stopped him midtirade, before he even had a chance to get warmed up. He felt, suddenly, as if he'd caught a deer in his headlights. "You're scared."

"Don't be ridic—" She thought better of that. "I am not."

"Oh, yes, you are." He reached out and caught her chin in his hand. "Look at me," he said, when she lowered her gaze. "Unless you're too scared to," he taunted when she refused to comply.

She lifted her lids and glared at him, her eyes shooting sparks of defiance that didn't quite hide the truth of his accusation.

"You're scared spitless."

She jerked her chin out of his hand and stood. "You're imagining things."

"Is it me?"

"Ha!"

"No, of course, it's not me," he said to himself. "If you were scared of me, I'd never have gotten in the door." He turned, still on his knees, a considering expression in his eyes as he watched her snatch her dress up off of the floor, turning it this way and that as she searched for the neck and armholes. "It's what I said, isn't it? It's the *L* word. You didn't start acting like a crazy woman until I mentioned the word *love.*"

"If anyone's acting crazy, it's you. We've known each other two days. Two days!" She yanked the dress over her head, discovered it was on backward and pulled her arms back inside, frantically trying to twist it around the right way. Her hands were shaking, making the process more difficult than it would normally be. "People don't fall in love in two days."

"I did." He reached out and grabbed a handful of fabric, impeding her movements as she struggled to straighten the dress. "I fell in love with you the first minute I saw you." He knew as soon as he said it that he'd never spoken truer words. He was ass-end-over-teakettle in love with her and had been since... Good, God, had it started when he saw the snapshot of her? Is that why he'd taken on a job he didn't really want?

Andie quit tugging on the dress and stood stock-still, her arms still inside the voluminous circle of fabric. Her mouth opened but no sound came out. It was just shock, she assured herself, as something warm and dangerously thrilling zinged through her. Shock that a grown man could say such a thing with a straight face.

"Oh, come on," she scoffed, when she could speak again. "Love at first sight? That only happens in the movies."

"Not only in the movies. I love you, Andrea."

Oh, God, she loved the way he called her Andrea! The way he looked at her when he said it. The sound of his voice as he uttered her name. No one except her family called her Andrea anymore. She'd become Andie to the outside world. Efficient, competent, sexless Andie. Andrea was a whole other woman. One she wasn't sure she knew anymore. One she wasn't sure she wanted to be.

"Did you hear what I said? I love you."

"No you don't." She got her arms through the correct openings and reached down with both hands, yanking at the full skirt to pull it out of his grip. "It's just the sex talking, is all. Great sex makes people think they feel all kinds of crazy things. But no matter how wonderful it is, it doesn't equal love. It just... Stop looking at me like that."

"Like what?"

She took a careful step back. "Like you're thinking of pulling me down on the floor again."

"You said the sex was great."

"Until you dragged sentiment into it, it was. No." She took another quick step back, avoiding his hand. "Get up off the floor. You look ridiculous down there."

Actually, he looked...too good. He looked gorgeous. And sweet. And devastatingly sexy. She was almost tempted to throw caution to the wind and get back down on the floor with him, except she knew he'd take it the wrong way. The crazy fool thought he was in love with her! And having sex with him again would only encourage him in his delusion.

Jim stayed where he was. "It makes you nervous, doesn't it?" His mouth quirked up at one corner. "Me on my knees in front of you? It scares you to death."

The smile spread, turning into a grin as he suddenly began to see the humor in the situation. They'd reversed roles again. *He* was the one who was supposed to shy away from commitment, who was supposed to be giving the speech about sex not equaling love. *She* was supposed to be the one getting all misty eyed and sentimental, weaving little happily-ever-after scenarios in her mind.

"Afraid I'll propose while I'm down here?"

That sent her into a near panic. "Fine." She settled the dress around her with a sharp tug. "Stay there. I'm going to reheat the pizza." She grabbed the pizza tray off of the table and stomped into the kitchen.

Jim got to his feet and followed her. "Your husband really did a number on you, didn't he?"

"Ex-husband," she snapped, as she fiddled with the oven controls. "And, no, he did not do a number on me. I'm just not interested in any kind of permanent relationship, is all. I like my freedom."

"I haven't asked you to give it up." *Yet*.

"And I *don't* like it when the rules change midstream." She opened the oven door and slid the pizza inside.

"I didn't know there were any rules," he grumbled. "Nobody told me about any rules."

"I thought this was going to be a simple, no-strings-attached affair and then you go and...and..." She couldn't bring herself to say it.

Jim had no problem with the words. "Fall in love with you," he finished for her.

"*Stop saying that!*" She jerked up, inadvertently slamming the oven door, and whirled around.

He was right behind her, crowding her, as naked as the day he was born. And aroused. Blatantly, fully, beautifully aroused.

She put her hands on his shoulders and pushed. "Go put your clothes on," she said, an edge of desperation in her voice. He was hard enough to resist fully clothed. Naked, his appeal was lethal.

He reached up and captured her hands, dragging them down against his chest.

She backed away from him and bumped into the stove.

"Careful there." He transferred his hands to her waist, shifting her a little farther down the counter, out of harm's way. "Don't burn yourself."

Too late, she thought. She was already on fire, burning up from the inside out. But she couldn't give in to the heat. Not now. Not again. Not with the *L* word hanging in the air between them. It wouldn't be fair. "This isn't a good idea. We really shouldn't be— Umm...." She sighed as he bent his head and nuzzled her neck. "Oh, ye—no." She tilted her head away from him. "No, don't."

"Why not?" He ran his tongue up the side of her arched neck to her ear, smiling to himself when he felt her shiver. "Since you're only using me for sex, you might as well take full advantage of every opportunity."

"I...oooh...it's not just the sex," she managed to say breathlessly.

"It's not?"

"No. I'm, uh..." She tilted her head the other way, giving him access to her other ear. "I'm..."

He obliged her by nipping her lobe. "You're what?"

"I'm fond of you."

He drew back a little to look at her. "*Fond* of me?" he said with a grimace.

"Yes," she said seriously. "I like you. I like you a lot. That's why I don't think we should do this again. It wouldn't be fair to you."

"What wouldn't be fair to me?"

"*This*. Having sex again."

"You want to explain that?"

"I don't want to take advantage of the way you feel."

"Wait a minute. Let me get this straight." The golden lights in his eyes twinkled with sudden amusement. "*You* don't want to take advantage of *me*?"

Andie nodded. "That's right."

"And you think it would be taking advantage of me to have sex again?"

"Yes," she said, glad he understood.

"Because...?"

Well, maybe he didn't understand, after all. Men were notoriously slow-witted when it came to the nuances of emotion. "Because you lo—" She still couldn't bring herself to utter the word. "Because of the way you said you feel about me," she explained patiently. "Having sex now would..." She shrugged uneasily. "It might make you think there's a chance I'll return your feelings." Her eyes were wide and serious. "I won't."

That should have hurt, Jim thought, but curiously, it didn't. Or at least not as much as it might have even a few minutes ago. She might want to believe it was just sex, but he knew better. A woman didn't fall into bed with a man after eight years of celibacy because she was *fond* of him. She didn't melt at his slightest touch because she *liked* him. Those were lukewarm emotions, and there was nothing lukewarm about her response to him. What she felt for him was so strong it frightened her. It frightened her so much that she had to deny it even existed.

He vowed to tread carefully from here on in. To take it slowly. To lull her into acceptance of what was between them.

"I think it's sweet that you're worried about my feelings, but it isn't necessary. I'm a big boy. I can take care of myself."

"I just don't want to lead you on."

"How could you be leading me on?" he asked, and then didn't wait for the answer. "You've told me exactly how you feel. You've been completely honest. That's all anyone can ask for."

"But—"

"But, nothing." He ran his hands lightly up and down her sides, from her waist to the outer curve of her breasts and back again, leaving ripples of gooseflesh in his wake. "My feelings are my responsibility, not yours."

"But—"

He pulled her hips against him, nudging her with his erection. "Do you really want me to leave?"

"I..." She should send him away. She knew she should. For his good and her own. It would be the smart thing to do. The right thing.

He found her nipples through the thin cotton of her dress and pinched them lightly. "Do you?"

Andie sucked in her breath. "No," she breathed, and silently cursed her weakness. "No. I don't want you to leave."

His smile was all triumphant male. "Good," he murmured, "because I wasn't going to go, no matter what you said."

He wrapped his arms around her and bent his head, taking her mouth with his before she could utter another word or think to protest his arrogance. She responded immediately, passionately, sliding her arms under his, palms flat against the hard curve of his spine, holding tight as her head fell back under the onslaught of his lips. They kissed as if it were the first time—or the last. Hungrily, mouths open, straining together as if they hadn't found ecstasy in each other's arms just a short time before. She could feel the edge of the kitchen counter pressing into the small of her back, his erection, hard and insistent, pushing against the softness of stomach. His bare chest flattened her breasts.

She murmured and shifted against him, going up on tiptoe, trying to get closer, running her hands down the long, smooth muscles of his back to his narrow hips. She felt the raised welt of the scar from his accident, barely registering it as her palms curved over his tight little rear end. He really did have sweet cheeks.

He changed the angle of the kiss, taking it deeper, holding her tighter, trying to brand her with his taste and his smell and the feel of his body against hers. He wanted to inundate her with his essence, imprint himself into her very bones, into the synapses of her brain cells, until all she could see, all she could feel, all she could think of was him and the way he made her feel. He knew what she liked now—what made her sigh; what made her squirm; what made her moan and melt and grow moist; what made her scream with pleasure. He lifted her onto the kitchen counter and ruthlessly, deliberately began to use his intimate knowledge of her.

She liked to be bitten, lightly. He obliged her, feasting oh so gently on her tender flesh, nipping carefully at her lower lip, her earlobes, the tender spot at the base of her neck, the curve of her shoulder.

She liked to have her nipples pinched, very delicately. He did so, first with his fingertips, then with his lips and teeth, dampening her bodice, sucking and nibbling at her breasts until they were hard and pointy.

She liked a steady, circular pressure against her pubis. He pressed the heel of his hand between her legs, over the billowing fabric of her dress, and rotated it slowly, nerve-rackingly slowly, until she moaned and began gathering the hem in her own hand, pulling it up so he could touch the bare, moist folds of her.

He wanted to tell her he loved her. Wanted to whisper it over and over, *ached* to say it. But he knew it would panic her again. She had to experience it on a more basic level first. She had to feel it in his touch and taste it on his lips. She had to perceive it subliminally, through her pores and nerve endings, to know it was true at her core, before she would trust the words.

In a blinding flash of insight, he realized he wasn't going to earn her trust the way he was going about it. He wasn't going to make her feel loved by groping her on a kitchen counter, or taking her on the floor or up against the wall again. A woman needed tenderness to feel loved. She needed softness and sweetness and romance. She needed to feel cherished and adored. All he'd done so far was to overwhelm her with passion and technique, to prove the truth of her assertion that it was just sex. How could she think otherwise when every time he got near her he turned into a raving sex maniac? He'd shown her he lusted after her. It was time—past time—to show her that he loved her, too. And to make her believe it.

She murmured a confused protest when he withdrew his hand from between her legs, then she reached out blindly, trying to direct his touch back to where she needed it most. He caught her hands in his, lifting them to his shoulders, and slid one arm around her back. She shifted eagerly to accommodate him, scooting forward on the counter to wrap her legs around his waist and take him inside her.

But instead he slid his other arm under her knees, kissing her temple as he swept her off of the counter and into his arms.

She uttered another protest, a wordless sound of thwarted desire, and nipped at his shoulder.

"No." He tightened his arms and cradled her closer, like a beloved and cherished child, pressing another kiss to the corner of her eye when she squirmed. "No, baby," he murmured. "Not yet. Wait."

And, inexplicably, Andie was soothed. She twined her arms around his neck and laid her head on his shoulder, silently willing him to do what he would with her. In his own way. In his own time.

She was so tired of standing on her own two feet, of being in charge and running the show, so tired of being supercompetent Andie Wagner. Tonight, just for tonight, she'd be Andrea again, she'd let someone else make all the decisions and set the pace, to lead her to where they both wanted to go. Tomorrow morning would be soon enough to take back control and deal with the consequences.

And she knew there would be consequences. She'd known it from the start, even before he'd uttered the dreaded *L* word.

Except, here she was being carried up the stairs to her

bedroom, cradled in the strong, sheltering arms of the only man she had wanted since...well, since far too long before her divorce. And it was her good fortune that this man she wanted so desperately was a man who was as intent on giving pleasure as on getting it, with no hang-ups about who gave and who got, who took and who received, who did and who was done to. With him, she didn't have to worry about appearing unfeminine or not being sexy enough. She didn't have to worry about being too aggressive, or too intelligent, or too demanding. He hadn't been offended or shocked by anything she'd done. He'd been strong enough and confident enough to let her take the lead in their lovemaking. Now it was time to return the favor. If he wanted her to take the passive role this time, to play the helpless maiden to his strong, conquering male, well, he'd earned it. And she trusted him enough to believe he wouldn't mistake her surrender for weakness.

He set her on her feet by the bed and she stood docilely, her dress brushing against her calves, watching as he neatly and efficiently folded the quilted comforter to the foot of the bed and propped the pillows up against the white wicker headboard. He turned to her and gently, silently, stripped her out of her dress, kissing each shoulder as he lowered the straps, taking her hand to help her step out of it as it pooled around her feet. He scooped her back up into his arms then, still without saying a word, and laid her on the turned-down bed. She expected him to come over her then, to lower himself into her arms and into her body, but he pressed a soft kiss on her forehead and straightened away from her. She lay quietly, acquiescent, her body relaxed and waiting, watching him as, naked and completely at ease, he moved around her bedroom.

He picked up her dress off the floor, shook it out and draped it over the back of the wicker chair in the corner. He closed the drapes and turned on the small lamp on her dresser, tilting the shade so that the light was diffused against the wall, leaving the room bathed in shadows. Only then, when he had done what he could to set the scene for romance, did he return to the bed.

And the woman on it.

He sat on the edge of the bed, the hard curve of his hip touching hers, taking her hands in his when she reached for him, bringing them to his lips to kiss and caress. Andie curled her fingers, instinctively trying to hide her callused palms from such close scrutiny, but he wouldn't allow it.

"You have beautiful hands." He pressed soft, open-mouthed kisses against the ridge of hardened skin at the base of her fingers and tickled her palm with his tongue. "Strong hands. Capable hands." He cupped the backs of them in his and held them to his face, rubbing against her palms like a huge cat, asking to be petted.

Andie obliged him, her hands conforming to the hard planes of his cheeks, her fingers sliding into his thick, glossy hair, kneading his scalp as he turned his head one way, then the other, to kiss the pulse beating beneath the delicate skin of each wrist. She sighed as he skimmed his hands down the backs of her arms, lightly caressing, preparing the way for kisses that rambled down her forearms to the sensitive flesh at the inside of her elbows, and on to the curve of her shoulder. She tilted her head back against the pillows, lifting her chin, baring her throat for more of his soft seduction.

He took advantage of her generosity, bending over to nibble at her collarbone and nuzzle his face into the curve of her neck. He traced the delicate whorls of one ear, then the other, with the tip of his tongue, planting tiny little baby kisses all along her jaw and across her chin as he moved from left to right and back again. "You've got the sweetest, daintiest little ears," he whispered.

Andie shivered and sighed. Her body softened. Her hands fell from his hair to lay, as open and defenseless as flower petals, against the yellow-striped sheets. Her eyes drifted closed as she surrendered and gave herself up to him.

Just that and no more, he thought, awed by her response. Just a tender touch and a soft, caressing word and that fierce, iron will of hers was quieted and subdued. He felt honored. And humbled. It made him feel powerful and weak, all at once. Mostly, it made him want to give her more. So much more.

He lifted his legs onto the bed and propped himself up on one elbow beside her, sliding his palm under her head, cradling it, turning her face to his. "You've got the most gorgeous skin," he murmured as he brushed his lips across her forehead and temples, over her eyelids and the tip of her nose and her flushed cheeks. "Just like a baby's. So soft and silky. All over." He trailed his other hand down her torso, his fingertips lightly skimming over breast and belly and thigh before coming back to curve around her throat. "And your mouth." He pushed her chin up with his thumb. "It's perfect." He pressed a lingering kiss to each corner. "And this sexy little scar—" he brushed his index finger back and forth across the tiny raised white line beneath her lower lip "—drives me crazy."

Andie opened wondering eyes to look up at him. "Sexy?"

"Very sexy." He flicked at her chin with his tongue, lapping at her as if she were a particularly delicious ice-cream cone. "It makes you look just a little bit danger-ous. And mysterious. I keep wondering how you got it."

"I whacked myself in the mouth with a hammer about six years ago, when I was trying to remove a bent nail from a stud. Not very dangerous." A small, self-mocking smile flickered across her face for a moment. "Except to myself."

"It's still sexy." He pressed his lips to the tiny scar. "Incredibly sexy. It makes me hot just to look at it." His eyes blazed, shards of gold gleaming in the dim light. "Everything about you makes me hot. Your skin. Your mouth. Your eyes. Your perfume. Your perfume drives me totally around the bend. Especially when you put it on this sweet little spot, right here." He moved his hand, skimming it along her collarbone, cupping her shoulder, pressing his mouth against the love bite he'd placed on her neck the night before. "You have won-derful shoulders, too. I thought so the first time I saw you standing there in the entry hall at Belmont House in that little sleeveless undershirt. They're so strong and smooth and sleek. And your breasts. Ah, Andrea, your pretty little breasts are a work of art."

He worked his way down her body, slowly, caressing her with hot, gentle hands and languorous, open-mouthed kisses and soft words of praise and celebration that asked nothing in return except that she accept and enjoy.

"You're so delicate. So fragile," he marveled as he smoothed his palm over her small, pink-crested breasts and narrow rib cage, down the slope of her waist and the gentle flare of her hips to the long, taut muscles of her thighs. "And yet so strong. So sleek and curvy and sexy as all hell."

Andie had never felt so passionately desired, so unconditionally adored, so utterly sheltered and safe as she did in this man's arms. He stroked her flesh and inflamed her senses and touched her carefully guarded heart with his tender wooing. She was weak with longing, on fire for his total possession, and yet so utterly content, so completely enchanted by what he was doing and saying, that she didn't feel the usual need to urge him, beg him, to hurry, and take her. She didn't turn her head to capture his lips for a deeper kiss, she didn't writhe against him, she didn't flex her hips against his hand in a wordless demand for more. He would get to it, she knew. And if he didn't, well...she was strangely content with that, too. In this moment, she trusted him to take care of her; to fulfill her every desire; to know intuitively exactly what she needed—and how and when—better than she knew herself.

And when, finally, he rose up over her and parted her legs, her last coherent thought before he entered her was that maybe—just maybe—falling in love again might not be so bad, after all.

10

"OH, NO. NO." Andie came to a dead stop on the threshold of the front door of Belmont House, one hand still on the doorknob, the other holding the key she had just taken out of the dead-bolt lock. "Damn it. *No!*"

Standing behind her, his hands on her shoulders, his head bent to plant a quick, playful kiss on the nape of her neck before the official start of the workday, Jim didn't have to ask her what had made her utter the first swear word he'd ever heard out of her mouth. The cause of her distress was smeared all across the two-story foyer wall in bright red paint, over and over again.

I warned you, Bitch. Ball-buster. Whore. Jezebel.

"But the front door was locked! Double locked." She turned to face him, as if she needed eye-to-eye contact to convince him—and herself—of that fact. "You stood right there and watched me unlock it. I had to use two different keys."

"There are other doors," he reminded her.

"They're all locked, too. All four of them. I made sure of that before I left last night."

"Obviously, this slimeball doesn't have any more respect for locked doors than he does for female construction workers." Jim squeezed her shoulders and stepped around her. "You go on out to your truck and wait. I want to see which lock he broke to get in."

Andie wasn't waiting anywhere, for anyone. This was her business. Her livelihood. Her problem. She stuffed the keys into the pocket of her overalls and brushed past Jim, heading for the French doors in the dining room, which would be the easiest place for someone to break into the house.

The doors were intact and securely locked. No windows had been broken to gain entry. But the crystal chandelier had been used as a piñata. Most of the remaining prisms had been shattered, leaving fragments of glass scattered like stardust across the hardwood floor. A crowbar hung from the once elegant fixture, its curved claw caught in the mangled wiring. All Andie could think, just then, was that she was glad she hadn't had time to order the replacement prisms because now she was going to have to get a whole new chandelier.

"Don't touch it." Jim's voice stopped her as she reached for the crowbar. "Don't touch anything. There may be fingerprints."

Andie's hands curled into fists, but she nodded, silently acknowledging the wisdom of his advice. She backed away from the ravaged chandelier. Dry-eyed and tight-lipped with fury, she turned and headed toward the matching set of French doors in the library on the opposite side of the house.

"Hold on a minute." Jim grabbed her arm, stopping her. He wanted to take her into his arms and tell her everything was going to be all right, but he knew she wouldn't appreciate it. She'd probably bite his head off if he tried it. And she wouldn't believe him, anyway, because things weren't all right. "You can't go storming around like Rambo. The perp might still be here, waiting for you."

Andie yanked a pipe wrench out of her tool belt. "I hope he is."

"Oh, for cryin' out loud. What do you think you're going to do with that?" She looked like a small, fierce kitten with her claws unsheathed, valiant and ridiculous at the same time. He wanted to take her in his arms again, to protect her and shelter her. He settled for snatching the makeshift weapon out of her hand. "Anybody could take this away from you as easily as I just did. And then where would you be?"

She glared at him.

"It's time to call the police, Andrea."

"I have to check the rest of the house first."

"Let the police do it. That's what they're paid for."

"I have to see for myself first," she insisted, not wanting anyone to witness her reaction when she did.

"All right." He recognized an immovable object when he saw one. Recognized, too, that she was hanging on to control by a thread. Taking a look around first, before they called the police, wouldn't hurt anything. Despite what he'd said to her, the perpetrator was undoubtedly long gone. "All right, we'll look first. But stay behind me." He stepped in front of her and started back across the wide foyer to the other side of the house. "And put your hands behind your back so you don't forget and accidentally touch something."

The French doors in the library were intact, as was the sturdy servants' entrance in the kitchen and the small side door that led out to the conservatory. They found the point of entry upstairs in the master bedroom. The perpetrator had broken a window, the tall curved one that opened out onto the scaffolding that had been erected to repair the brickwork on the tower.

Ugly spray-painted epitaphs were smeared across the freshly plastered walls and the newly restored fireplace.

Bitch. Whore. Jezebel.

"Thank God the wallpaper isn't up yet," Andie said fervently. The walls could be replastered, the fireplace refinished and all it would cost her was time, but the antique-silk moiré wallpaper would have been irreplaceable except at a crippling cost to her budget.

"Andrea?"

At the sound of Jim's voice she looked up, wresting her gaze and her attention from the paint-smeared marble mantel. He was standing in the doorway between the master bedroom and the sitting room. And something in his eyes made her stomach contract with sudden dread. She hurried across the room, intending to brush past him to see for herself what had put that look on his face. He wrapped his fingers around her slender biceps, holding her there beside him, not letting her go any farther, as if wanting to protect her from what lay on the other side of the threshold.

But nothing could protect her from what had already happened.

There were ugly words sprayed on the bare walls in the sitting room. She'd expected that. But worse, much worse, were the overturned crates that held the hand-painted tiles for the master bathroom. Packing material spilled out over the floor. Smashed and broken tiles lay everywhere.

"Oh, God." Andie felt the rage and the fear and the hated sense of helplessness well up inside her. Her first instinct was to turn into the strong arms waiting to hold her, to bury her head against the hard male chest of her lover and howl. And because she wanted to do just that so desperately, she didn't. She had to act sensibly. She had to take control of the situation. She had to stand on her own two feet. Especially now, when all she wanted to do was lay her burden on Jim's broad shoulders and plead with him to take care of it for her, she *had* to be in charge.

She pulled away from him, holding herself rigid, clamping down on the emotions that threatened to overwhelm her. "You're right," she said calmly. Only her eyes, those crystal-clear windows into her soul, gave away the roiling emotions inside her. "It's time to call the police."

THE POLICE ARRIVED about the same time her crew did, causing a momentary traffic jam at the front door of Belmont House until someone from the force finally sorted things out and made the procedure clear.

"I want everyone to stay outside," the plainclothes detective ordered. "You'll all be interviewed as soon as we can get to you—" he motioned at the two uniformed police officers standing on the brick walkway "—so don't go anywhere." He offered a small, humorless smile over an oft-voiced quip. "It'll go smoother for everyone if we don't have to track you down. Ms. Wagner, if you'll come inside with me, please?"

Instinctively, without even realizing she was doing it, Andie looked around for Jim, wanting him by her side. He was standing on the sidewalk, being interviewed by another plainclothes officer. It was a standard police tactic to separate the witnesses to a crime before they could contaminate each other's version of the event; no two people saw anything in exactly the same way, and recollections were easily swayed. Andie turned and followed the detective up the front stairs and into the house, noting the two elderly people standing on the porch across the street, watching the proceedings.

Mr. and Mrs. Hastings were a lovely old couple and the neighborhood's main source of gossip. They "took the air" twice a day, once after luncheon and once after supper, gathering and transferring information like bees in a meadow. Andie had no doubt that by the time their afternoon walk was over, the whole story of what had happened at Belmont House would be common knowledge to residents on both sides of the street.

"Isn't all this just a little bit of overkill, Detective Coffey?" she said to the man she recognized as one of her father's former colleagues. Normally, only two uniformed officers would have been dispatched on a call like hers. Instead, there was a small army swarming over her job site, dusting for prints, taking pictures, interviewing her crew, making notes—which was part of the reason she'd been so reluctant to call the police in the first place. She'd known something like this would happen. "The neighbors are going to think there's a major drug bust going down, or that we found a couple of hacked-up bodies buried under the patio."

Detective Coffey just shrugged, tacitly admitting the truth of her words.

"And aren't you on vice now?" She knew she was being catty and ungrateful, but she couldn't seem to help it. Every nerve in her body was strung tight and her mind was racing every which way, trying to come up with a viable plan to replace the chandelier and the destroyed tiles and still bring the job in on time and under budget. She wanted to be inspecting the damage herself—right now!—instead of standing around answering questions with no real answers. "Shouldn't you be out chasing drug dealers and pimps instead of dealing with a simple case of trespass and vandalism?"

"I was in the squad room when your call came in," Coffey said. "I recognized your name."

"So, being that I'm the daughter of an old police buddy, you just had to take it on?"

"Whatever." Coffey took out a notebook and flipped it open. "I'm sure you know the drill, Ms. Wagner. You want to run over it for me?"

Knowing she wasn't going to accomplish anything by continuing to needle him, Andie took a deep breath, reaching deep for control, and "ran over it for him." Very calmly and concisely, she told him everything that had happened from the time she'd opened the front door to the moment she'd used the cell phone in her tool belt to call the police. Detective Coffey took every word down in his notebook as they walked through the crime scene, going over it step by step.

"And this has been going on for, what? One month? Two?"

"A little over two, on and off. But it's only been graffiti up to now."

"Just graffiti? That's it? No other communication?"

"Such as?"

"Mash notes left in your truck, say? Harassing phone calls? Anything like that?"

"No." She deliberately didn't mention the phone calls to her home because she didn't think they were related to what was going on at the work site. If her father knew about them, he'd go into overdrive, putting a tap on her phone line and having Coffey shadowing her every move. And she'd already taken every sensible precaution to handle it. "It's just been the graffiti. Which I'm sure you're aware of," she added, letting him know that she knew he'd been in touch with her father. "It's been annoying, but essentially harmless. There was no reason to call the police before today."

"And yesterday, when the chandelier was first damaged? Why didn't you call the police then?"

Andie eyed him suspiciously. "Who told you about that?"

Coffey shrugged. "I heard some talk about it outside."

Andie wasn't sure she believed that; she didn't think he'd been outside long enough to hear talk, but anything was possible. And where else would he have heard it?

"So, you want to tell me what happened yesterday?"

Andie told him.

"Any idea who the perp might be? Anybody got a grudge against you?"

Andie shook her head. "A lot of guys in this industry don't take kindly to women in construction. Especially women who run their own companies. I got an outraged phone call from one of the men I beat out for this job. And a nasty note from another."

"I thought you said there hadn't been any other communications?"

"This was months ago, after the bid was first awarded and competition fever was still running a little high. I haven't heard a thing from either of them since."

"Uh-huh." Coffey made a note. "You said the note was nasty? Nasty how?"

"Not sexual, if that's what you mean. The first guy

accused me of being a substandard contractor because I was a woman, and said I only got this job because of quotas and affirmative action. The one who wrote the note vented about women stepping out of their rightful roles and taking jobs away from men who were the real breadwinners. I really don't think either one of them has anything to do with this, detective. They were both up-front. Angry, but up-front. Not anonymous like—" she gestured at the spray-painted wall. Her lip curled disdainfully "—him."

"Why don't you give me their names, anyway?" Coffey suggested.

Andie reluctantly gave him the names, knowing that having the police come down on her competitors would be another black mark against her, because she couldn't "take it like a man."

"How about old boyfriends? You dump anyone recently?"

"I don't think that's relevant. This is professional, not personal."

"Calling someone a ball-busting bitch might— *might*—" he emphasized, "be motivated by professional jealousy. But men don't usually throw around words like *whore* and *Jezebel* unless they're feeling personally involved. So just answer the question, will you? Any old boyfriends hanging around who might still be carrying a torch?"

"I assure you, Detective, you're barking up the wrong tree here. I don't have any boyfriends, old or otherwise. And this *is* strictly professional. Women in construction get this kind of harassment all the time. If some bozo's not calling you a lesbian, he's calling you a slut. Attacking a woman's sexuality is a time-honored way of trying to keep her in line. I'd think you'd know that."

"Granted. But this feels like more than just run-of-the-mill harassment. This guy is twisted." He tapped the side of his nose with his index finger. "I can smell it."

"Detective Coffey has a valid point," Jim said from behind her. "This whole thing is beginning to feel real personal to me, too."

Andie turned her head to look at him, torn between being pleased to have him by her side and annoyed that he'd agreed with Detective Coffey.

"I think you're both wrong," she said firmly, and watched the two of them exchange a superior man-to-man look, commiserating over the little lady's wrong-headedness. It got Andie's back up and set her nerves to silently screaming again. "But I can also see that you've already made up your minds and nothing I say is going to change them." Her voice dripped ice. Her eyes flashed fire. "I'll leave you gentlemen to discuss your fascinating theory between yourselves. I've got better things to do."

"Excuse me. Detective...ah, Coffey." One of the uniformed officers, a young woman in her mid-twenties, interrupted them before Andie could take her leave. "We've finished dusting for prints."

"And?"

Andie stood riveted to the floor, waiting for the answer.

"There aren't any."

"None?" Jim asked before Coffey could.

The young officer turned to face him. "None that are useful, sir. The banister and the scaffolding, both inside and out, are covered with prints, but it's going to take us a while to match them all up and weed out the ones of the people who work here, plus tradespeople and the like. And I don't think it'll be worth it. There are too many people and too many prints involved."

"I figured that would probably be the case," Jim said. "But it was worth a try."

Coffey nodded, silently signaling his agreement. "Anything else?"

"Not much, sir. The crowbar in the dining room and that empty can of spray paint we found under the scaffolding downstairs have been wiped clean. Not so much as a partial. Same for the windowsill in the bedroom. I'd say it's a pretty good bet the perp wore gloves."

"Pro?" Coffey said. He was looking at Jim.

Jim shrugged. "Could be he just watches a lot of cop shows on TV."

Coffey grunted and indicated that the young woman should continue with her report.

"Officer Benson took a couple of shots of the boot prints in the glass and the dust from the smashed tiles," she said. "There are more boot prints outside, but it's kind of the same situation as with the fingerprints—lots of people in work boots and all of them with a legitimate reason to be tramping around the site. But we found this—" she held up a plastic bag "—on the floor next to one of the overturned crates. I figure he might have cut himself when he broke the window."

"That won't do you any good," Andie said, gesturing at the bag the officer handed to Coffey. "That bandanna's mine. I gouged my knuckles yesterday—" she held up her hand to show them "—and used it as a temporary bandage."

"Any idea how it got on the floor in the other room?"

"That was my doing," Jim said easily. "I insisted Andrea—that is, Ms. Wagner—let me clean her wound and put on a proper bandage."

"And you just dropped the bandanna on the floor when you were finished with it?" Coffey shook his head. "Pretty careless, contaminating the crime scene like that." He sighed heavily. "Now we have to catalog it. Let the lab boys have a look at it." He nodded at the young officer, dismissing her.

"Jim didn't have anything to do with this," Andie said, when the young officer was out of earshot. She knew how cops' minds worked. They took a tiny piece of insignificant evidence and immediately started putting two-and-two together—and getting five. "He was, ah..." It pained her to have to admit it, knowing it would get back to her father. And, besides, her private life was just that. Private. She didn't like discussing it with strangers, but she didn't want Detective Coffey jumping to the wrong conclusions, either. "Jim was with me last night," she said, her expression daring him to make anything of it. "All night."

"Hey." Coffey lifted one shoulder in a careless shrug and flipped his notebook closed. "Nobody's accusing anybody of anything." He flashed another look at Jim, one that Andie couldn't quite decipher. Not quite suspicion. Not quite doubt. There was a hint of speculation in the look. A subtle warning, perhaps. And, unbelievably, a trace of humor. "'Course, the lieutenant might think otherwise," he added, referring to Andie's father as if he were still on the force.

AFTER THE POLICE LEFT, Andie didn't waste any time getting everyone back to work. "Time is money, people," she said briskly, refusing to feel sorry for herself or think about what had happened. If she took even a moment, the floodgates would open and she'd embarrass herself by going on a crying jag in front of her crew. "And we don't have enough of either to waste right now. Mary, Tiffany, you two take care of the damaged chandelier and clean up the broken glass in the dining room. When you're finished with that, I want you to see about getting an alarm system for this place. I want it noisy—something that'll wake the dead when it goes off—and I want it installed today. Dot, you're in charge of fixing the broken window in the master bedroom. Pete, you take Jim and Matthew and get busy cleaning the paint off the walls and fireplace. Booker, you can give me a hand in the sitting room," she said. "I need you to help me with the crates."

"I'll help you with those," Jim said, modifying her instructions without a second thought. "Booker can work with Pete and Matthew."

"*No.*" She snapped out the word as if she was a bad-tempered drill sergeant.

Everyone stopped in their tracks and turned to look at her. They were used to Andie being firm about what she wanted done, that was no surprise, but she was usually polite about it. Her orders were always couched as requests. And she didn't yell.

"I've given you all your work orders for today." Her steely gaze touched everyone in turn—except Jim. "So let's all get to it, shall we?"

Only Booker and Jim failed to scurry away to do her bidding.

Booker stood in the middle of the foyer unsure of what to do, his gaze darting back and forth between Andie and Jim.

"Booker." Andie cocked her head toward the stairs, indicating that he should do what he'd been told. "You head on up to the sitting room and start getting rid of the broken tile. I'll be there in a minute." She waited until he was out of earshot before she finally looked at Jim. "I'd appreciate it if you wouldn't countermand my orders in front of the crew," she said stiffly, holding on to control by a delicate thread. "If you have a problem with your work assignment for the day, I'd prefer you discuss it with me in private."

"It's not my work assignment I have a problem with," he said mildly, watching her as if she were a bomb that might go off any minute. "It's you. Are you all right?"

"I'm fine."

"You're not fine. You're strung tighter than a junkie looking for his next fix. Talk to me, Andrea." He moved forward as he spoke and reached out for her. "Let me help you."

She stepped back, avoiding his touch. "I don't need any help."

He let his hand drop back to his side. "Everyone needs help once in a while. Life is too hard to deal with alone."

"I don't need any help," she repeated stubbornly. "I don't want any help."

The truth was she wanted it too much, and it scared her. It scared her exactly the same way hearing him say "I love you" scared her. She had no intention of getting into the habit of depending on him—not for love, not for help, not for *anything*—because, in the end, the only person a smart woman could really depend on was herself.

"All right. My mistake. You don't need any help." Jim struggled to keep the anger and hurt out of his voice. Struggled to be understanding. She was under a lot of pressure right now, both professionally and personally, and she was scared. He could see it in her eyes, in the rigid set of her shoulders and the way she pressed her soft lips together to keep them from trembling. She was trying desperately to keep it all together, to keep the fears and uncertainties inside and present a calm front to the world. He knew how that was. He also knew that, sooner or later, you had to let it out or you would shatter into a million screaming pieces.

"I'm not going to push it now," he said softly, carefully keeping his hands at his sides because he suspected—rightly—that it wouldn't take much just then to splinter her tenuous hold on control. "You've got enough to deal with at the moment, and now isn't the time or the place to go into it. But make no mistake, Andrea, there will be a time and a place. And we will talk about this. Soon."

Andie knew that by "this" he didn't just mean what had happened that morning at Belmont House. He didn't just mean the vandalism and its consequences and her reaction to it.

He meant they would talk about *them*.

Andie couldn't decide if that was a promise or a threat.

"I CAN'T BELIEVE IT. Hardly any of the tiles are actually broken," Andie said, nearly light-headed with relief at the discovery. It felt as if a crushing weight had been lifted off of her chest. Suddenly, she could breathe again. "Whoever did this must have just dumped the crates on their sides and smashed the tiles that fell out. He didn't go digging through the packing material for the ones that stayed in the crates." She blinked hard and bit her lip, struggling to hold back the tears that fear and anger hadn't been able to draw from her. "And, thank God, most of them stayed in the crates."

"So it's not as bad as you thought, then?" Booker said, watching her anxiously.

"No. No, it isn't."

Replacing the damaged chandelier and broken tiles was still going to take a sizable chunk out of her financial cushion, true, but it wasn't the catastrophe she had feared. She could manage it. If she could get the replacement tiles in a reasonable amount of time, if the alarm system she installed this afternoon didn't cost an arm and a leg, if nothing else went wrong she'd still be able to bring the job in on time and under budget.

She flashed her hovering apprentice a big smile that had his ears turning red. "It's not nearly as bad as I thought."

"HEY, GUYS." Andie smiled at the two workers who stood on the very top level of the scaffolding in the foyer, cleaning red paint off the wall with paint thinner and rags. From her position at the top of the staircase, they were catty-corner across the width of the foyer, about fifteen feet away and ten feet above her. "Either of you know where Jim is?"

Pete gave his usual monosyllabic grunt, which could have meant anything, then gestured toward the floor.

Andie leaned over the banister, through the networking of bars and boards that made up the scaffolding. "Jim?"

"Yeah?" He poked his head out from between two crossed bars, looking up at her from under the rim of a yellow hard hat. "What is it?"

She smiled at him and headed down the stairs.

He dropped the paint-smeared rag he'd been using and stepped out from under the scaffolding, reaching out to take her hands in his as she moved toward him. "You're feeling better about things. What happened?"

Andie beamed up at him, not even realizing that her hands were curled in his. She didn't see Pete and Matthew stop work and lean over the scaffolding to stare down at them. She didn't see anything but Jim.

"Oh, Jim." She was as giddy as a child who'd just been given a pony for her birthday. "Jim, you'll never guess."

"Then tell me."

"Hardly any of the tiles were damaged! A hundred, maybe, but that's all. The rest of them are *fine.*"

"That's wonderful, sweetheart." He hugged her to him, delighted for her, delighted for himself. "That's just great."

She hugged him back, burying her face against his chest to hide her glittering eyes. His arms tightened around her possessively. Protectively. Joyfully. She might be reluctant to share her troubles with him, but she'd sought him out to share her relief and happiness. She'd come straight to him with her good news. That had to mean something, didn't it? It was certainly a step in the right direction. He cupped her face in his hand to turn it up to his, then stopped, surprised when he felt dampness against his fingertips. "Andrea?"

"It's all right. I'm not crying. Really." She lifted her head and smiled at him, blinking back the tears that threatened to fall and make a liar of her. "I'm just so relieved. And—and..."

"Happy?"

"Yes. Yes. It isn't a disaster, after all, and I'm *delirious* with happiness," she said extravagantly, and threw her arms around his neck.

Their lips meet in a celebratory kiss. Lightly, at first, and then harder and deeper, as they both took fire. In another minute it would be blazing out of control. In another minute it *was* out of control and they were clinging to each other as if they were standing in the middle of her bedroom instead of in the foyer on the job site, in plain view of anyone who cared to look. One of his hands was at the small of her back, the other behind her head, cradling her against him, protective and possessive, soothing and demanding all at once. Her arms were wrapped around his neck, her hands clenched in his hair. The two of them were oblivious to everything except the need to be close again after the earlier strain between them.

"Oh, Jim... Jim, I'm sorry I snapped at you," she murmured against his mouth between kisses. "But I was so worried and upset and I took it out on—"

"It's all right, baby. I understand. I shouldn't have pushed and—"

"I'm so glad you were here with me, so—"

There was a loud clanging noise and a warning shout, and Jim glanced up just in time to see a can of something come hurtling down off the scaffolding above their heads. He did a quick shuffle backward, yanking Andie with him, instinctively tucking her against his chest, holding her there with his hand cupped protectively over the crown of her head as he folded himself around her. There was a sharp, metallic bang as the can bounced against one of the bars, then a resounding thud, like a muffled explosion, as it hit the floor. The contents spewed out, fountainlike, splattering them from the thighs down.

"Jesus, Mary and Joseph!" Matthew's red head appeared over the bar at the top of the scaffolding, his eyes wide as he stared down at them.

"What the hell was that?" Jim roared.

"Can of paint thinner," Pete hollered down, as if they wouldn't know that by now.

"Man, it's a good thing you had your hard hat on," Matthew said. "You guys okay down there?"

Booker appeared at the top of the stairs. Tiffany and Mary materialized in the doorway of the dining room.

"What's going on out here?"

"Is everybody okay?"

"We're fine. It didn't hit us," Andie said. "Everything's all right."

"It is *not* all right—" Jim began, rattled at the thought that Andie might have been hit, but she shushed him.

"We're fine," she insisted, ignoring the interested stares of her crew as she pushed Jim toward the front door. "Everybody can go back to work. There was no harm done."

"No harm done?" Jim let himself be pushed through the door and out onto the porch, protesting all the way. "If that thing had hit you, your brains would be splattered all over the floor along with the paint thinner.

What the hell were they doing up there, anyway, that made it fall?"

"But it didn't hit me, or you, either, did it?" She put her fingers over his lips, stopping him in midtirade. "So there was no harm done."

No physical harm, anyway, she amended silently.

What *had* happened was that she and Jim had crossed over some kind of threshold in their relationship. Stepped over some invisible line that pushed what was between them just that much closer to a relationship, as opposed to an affair. And she'd been the one who'd taken the step forward. *She* had crossed the line. She'd been crossing it from the beginning. Maybe it was time to put aside her fears, at least for the moment, and take things one tiny step farther, to trust him just a tiny bit more. If they were going to have anything more than an affair, if there was some kind of relationship between them, she was going to have to let him into her life. She dove in.

"I'm driving up to Moose Lake on Saturday to spend the weekend with my kids. Would you like to come with me?"

11

ANDIE HADN'T BEEN SURE how her two youngest children would react to seeing her with a man; it had never happened before. She doubted they even had many memories of her with their father, let alone anyone else. They'd both been so young at the time of the divorce—Emily barely three years old and Christopher just turned six, and Kevin had been the kind of workaholic father who was seldom home. None of her three kids were used to sharing her with anything except her job. She'd been prepared for resentment, or wariness, or even rudeness from her offspring when she brought Jim along to share their precious weekend together.

To her relief, they thought he was cool.

Emily's romantic twelve-year-old heart was won over by nothing more than his dark good looks and sexy smile. Chris was impressed by the gleaming Harley-Davidson. Only her father seemed to reserve judgment.

"I heard you've got something going with him," Nathan Bishop said gruffly, nodding toward where Jim stood hip deep in Moose Lake, teaching Chris some of the finer points of staying upright on a sailboard.

Andie turned her head on the chaise lounge to look at him. "Yeah? Who says?"

"I never reveal my sources." Her father shot her a

glance from under his grizzled brows. "You know that."

Andie shrugged. "And I don't corroborate anonymous tips."

He sputtered and growled, muttering under his breath about uppity women and ungrateful daughters who didn't show their fathers the proper respect.

Andie ignored him, turning back to watch her son and her lover out in the water. Chris, at fifteen, looked all gangly and boyish and impossibly endearing next to Jim's taller, more muscular body. Chris was standing next to the sailboard, his hands on the mast of the downed sail, nearly chest deep in water that lapped the waistband of Jim's faded red swim trunks. Her son's head was cocked at an attentive angle as he listened to whatever Jim was telling him.

Jim stood with one hand flat on the sailboard, the other gesturing in the air, describing—she supposed—the basics of harnessing the wind for the purpose of flying across the water.

Chris nodded once, signaling his understanding, and Jim stepped back, steadying the board with one hand while her son hoisted himself up. There was a brief pause in his upward motion when Chris's life vest snagged on the foot strap, but Jim loosened it, and then the boy was suddenly on his feet, the boom in his hands, flying across the water. Jim tented his hand over his eyes and watched his protegé approvingly, calling out encouragement and instructions when the sail fluttered and threatened to go down again.

There was a loud sigh on Andie's right and she turned toward Emily and her precocious little friend Jennifer, who sat on the edge of the dock with their long bare legs dangling in the water. Emily was wearing ragged cut-off denim shorts over her hot pink tank suit. Jennifer had on a bright neon green bikini that Andie thought was too revealing and too sophisticated for a thirteen-year-old girl. She wondered briefly what the girl's mother was thinking, letting her out of the house like that.

"He sure is a hunk and a half," Jennifer said, and she wasn't looking at Chris. "Do you think he has a girlfriend?"

"I think my mom is his girlfriend." Emily glanced over her shoulder at Andie and grinned, her blue eyes dancing. "Aren't you, Mom?"

"Really, Mrs. Wagner?" Jennifer breathed. "Is he *really* your boyfriend?"

Andie pulled down her sunglasses with her index finger and looked over the top of them at the two girls, amused by the patent disbelief in Jennifer's eyes. Apparently, Jennifer found the odd pairing as incredible as Andie herself did.

"He might be. Or he might not," she added provocatively. "I haven't decided yet."

Her father harrumphed.

Emily giggled. "Oh, Mom."

"My mother told me it wasn't smart to keep a man waiting," Jennifer said. "She says men are easily distracted and there aren't enough good ones out there to begin with, so a woman can't be too choosy or she'll lose out."

"Oh, well..." Andie didn't know quite what to say to that. Surely mothers weren't still passing out that kind of advice to their daughters? "I don't think the situation is quite that desperate." She looked at her own daughter, who was staring at her worldly little friend as if she held the wisdom of the ages. *Uh-oh.* "Women can be as choosy as they want to be these days," she said, selecting her words with care. "They don't have to settle for just any man. They don't have to choose *any* man at all, if they don't want to."

"But then you'll be all alone," Jennifer said, "and you won't have anyone to take care of you or provide for your old age."

"My mom doesn't need anyone to take care of her," Emily said loyally. "She can take care of herself. And she isn't alone. She has me and Chris and Kyle and Grandpa and Aunt Natalie and Uncle Lucas and—" she waved one skinny arm "—lots of people."

Andie smiled in relief. Her daughter was a bright, independent girl with a mind of her own. One summer spent in the company of a thirteen-year-old throwback to the fifties wasn't going to warp her outlook. Still, just to be on the safe side, she'd be sure to slip in a few points on the importance of self-sufficiency when she had that talk with Emily about boys and kissing.

"Coffey told me," Andie's father said when the girls went back to talking between themselves.

Andie pushed her sunglasses back up on her nose, hiding her eyes and carefully schooling her features, trying not to look too smug at her father's capitulation. She'd known if she waited long enough his curiosity would get the best of him.

"Coffee?" she said politely, delighting in making it as difficult for him as possible because, all grumbling aside, he'd have been disappointed if she made it too easy. "That sounds great, Dad. I'd love some."

"Don't get cute with me, little girl. You know good

and well what I'm talking about. And it isn't something to drink. Coffey said it looked like you and Nicolosi—" he gestured out toward the water "—had something going." Two spots of red appeared on his tanned cheekbones. "Coffey also said you came right out and admitted you'd spent the night with him."

"And if I did?"

"Dammit, that's not what I—what I..." He sputtered over the words and the flush on his face deepened. He looked away from his daughter for a moment, then looked back, his features composed, his eyes narrowed with an expression he'd perfected after forty years of dragging confessions out of the scumbags and miscreants of Minneapolis. "Did you?"

"I don't think that's really any of your business," Andie said, unimpressed by his scowl, "but, yes, I did. And just so you'll know, I'm planning on doing it again."

"Not—" he bellowed, then lowered his voice, mindful of the two girls sitting within earshot on the end of the dock. "Not in my house, you're not."

"Of course not," Andie agreed easily, refusing to react to the implied insult. "I have the children to think of."

"You should have been thinking of them a few days ago, *before* you got yourself involved in a—" He broke off at the look on his daughter's face. "Well..." He shrugged. "Just before, is all."

"But I didn't ask you, did I? And I don't intend to, either."

"Dammit, little girl! You're a respectable woman. A mother. You shouldn't be carrying on like—like..."

"Like a woman?" she said, before her father could

say something they'd both regret. She sat up in her chaise lounge and swung her bare feet to the wooden dock, facing him. "Look at it this way, Dad. I'm only doing what you've been urging me to do for the past eight years."

"Doing what I...? I never urged you to do any such thing!"

"Sure, you have," Andie insisted, pressing her advantage. It was rare that she won a war of words with her father. He could usually out-bluster her. "Haven't you been telling me to find myself a man? Well..." She spread her hands, her expression the epitome of logic and reasonableness. "I found one."

"Is he going to marry you?"

Andie rolled her eyes. "The subject hasn't come up." *I love you, Andrea.* "And if it did, I'd say no." She wondered if that were still true. Yes, of course it was still true! What was she thinking? "I'm never getting married again," she said firmly, reminding them both of that fact.

"A woman needs a man to take care of her," Nathan said stubbornly, "especially a woman with children."

"Now you sound like *Jennifer's* mother," she said, trying to make him laugh. When he didn't, she, too, sobered. "I don't need a man to take care of me or my children, Dad. I can take care of all of us just fine." She reached out and touched her father's bare, knobby knee. "Emily understands that. Why can't you?"

"I just want you to be happy."

"I know, Dad. I know. And I am," she said, wondering why it felt like a lie. She got to her feet and leaned over, lifting his purple Viking cap to plant a quick kiss on the top of his head. "I expect this little heart-to-heart to be kept between the two of us," she said as she replaced the cap.

"Meaning?"

"Meaning I don't want you grilling Jim about this."

"A father's got a right to ask a man what his intentions are."

"It's not his intentions you have to worry about in this case, but mine. I have no intention of getting married again," she stated firmly, telling herself it was as true now as it had been in those awful days right after her divorce. "So you and Jim can just get that thought right out of your heads."

"Now, see here, little girl—"

"Don't little girl me, you old goat. I'm not sixteen anymore. I'm thirty-eight, and I'm telling you right now I don't want you asking questions or interfering, even if you think it's for my own good. Understood?"

He scowled at her. "Understood," he agreed reluctantly.

"Good." She tapped the bill of his cap, tilting it down over his eyes. "Come on, you two," she said to the girls, "it's time to get the coals started for dinner."

OF COURSE HE INTERFERED.

Andie came out of the bedroom she was sharing with her daughter to get a final glass of water before turning in for the night and saw Jim and her father through the kitchen window. They were sitting out on the deck, surrounded by the glow of several strategically placed citronella candles that had been lighted earlier to keep the mosquitoes at bay. Her father had a thin cheroot clamped between his teeth. Jim held a brandy glass cradled in his palm. At first glance, they looked relaxed, companionable even, but from their body language, she could tell the conversation was intense.

Her first instinctive reaction was to storm out of the house and over to the edge of the deck to grab her father by the ear and drag him inside, all the while giving him the sharp side of her tongue for breaking his promise to her. It was what her mother would have done. And what Natalie was still apt to do, given the right provocation. But Andie was a milder sort and, after a moment's reflection, she went with her second reaction.

If she went storming outside, her father would point out that she hadn't exacted a promise of noninterference from him. Rather, she had asked if he understood her position. And Jim was—as he'd said once before—a big boy. He was perfectly capable of taking care of himself; if he wasn't, well, that would pretty much solve her problem for her. A man who couldn't stand up to her father wouldn't be around for very long.

She set her glass upside down on the drain board and went back to bed, leaving them to work it out between themselves.

"Is HE REALLY your boyfriend, Mom?" Emily asked when they were snuggled together in bed. "No kidding?"

"He really is my boyfriend." She was amazed to hear herself say it, but there it was. "No kidding." She pressed a soft kiss to her daughter's temple. "How do you feel about that?"

Emily shrugged. "Okay, I guess," she said, after a minute. "He's nice. I like him. Chris likes him, too. We talked about it while we were doing the dishes after dinner. Chris said Jim doesn't talk to him like he's a dumb kid or anything. He said they talked about construction and stuff and how Chris might be old enough next year to work part-time, if you said it was okay, 'cause lots of boys start working in construction when they're sixteen. Chris asked him how he got those scars. You know, the ones that stick up above his bathing suit?"

"Oh?" Andie murmured encouragingly. She hadn't yet asked Jim about his scars, and she was at least as curious about them as her children.

"Uh-huh. Chris said Jim fell off a building and had to have an operation so he could walk again. He said his hip is practically all made of plastic and metal pins now, and hardly any bones at all. Sometimes it sets off the metal detectors at the airport when he goes through."

"He told Chris all that, did he?"

"Uh-huh." Emily fell silent for a moment, and Andie could almost feel her gearing up for something. "Mom?"

"What, darling?"

"Do you and Mr. Nicolosi...well..." Emily squirmed a bit, embarrassed to be talking face-to-face, as it were, about such an intimate subject with her mother. "Do you kiss and stuff?"

Andie hesitated, squirming inside herself, but she'd always been honest with her children. "Yes, we kiss and, um, stuff."

"Is it nice?"

"Yes, it's very nice."

"Are you going to marry him?"

"He hasn't asked me to marry him," she said, skirting the issue by avoiding it.

"But if he did ask you?" Emily persisted. "Would you?"

Andie had to take a minute to think about that. A week ago she'd have said no immediately, with no hesitation and no regret. Even yesterday she would have said no without a qualm. But now...? Now she wasn't *quite* as sure. Last week she'd have sworn she'd never have another lover, either. Yesterday she wouldn't have even acknowledged Jim Nicolosi as her boyfriend.

"No," she said at last, firmly, as much for her benefit as her daughter's. "No, I wouldn't. But..." She couldn't resist it, couldn't stop herself from asking. "How would you feel about it if I did?"

"Okay, I guess. He's nice. And you smile when you look at him." Emily snuggled closer to her mother, burrowing into the warmth and comfort of her body. "So, if you ever did want to marry him, it would be okay with me."

ANDIE TUGGED OFF her motorcycle helmet and hung it over the handlebar of the Harley, then threaded her fingers together and stretched, loosening the kinks, while Jim filled the motorcycle with gasoline for the return trip to Minneapolis late Sunday afternoon. "What did my father say to you?"

"What did he say to me when?" Jim asked, his eyes on the steadily mounting numbers on the gas pump.

"Out on the deck last night." She ran both hands through her flattened hair, fluffing it. "It looked like a pretty intense conversation."

"Oh, that." Jim shrugged. "He wanted to know what I knew about what's going on with the vandalism at your job site."

"He talked to you about that?"

"Yeah, sure. Why wouldn't he?" He returned the nozzle to the pump stand before he looked up at her. "I mean, I was there and all," he added hurriedly, alerted by the sudden flash of anger in her eyes. "He wanted a first hand repo—uh, account of someone who'd been there."

"Jeez, I should have known. He wanted a *man's* account. My firsthand report wasn't good enough." She threw up her hands, torn between exasperation and amusement. "And here I thought he was out there grilling you about something else entirely."

"What else would he be grilling me about?"

Andie shrugged, suddenly feeling just a little embarrassed. "Your intentions."

"My intentions?"

"Toward me." She waited a beat. "I told him we were sleeping together."

"You told him *what?*"

"That we're sleeping together," she repeated, and then laughed at his thunderstruck expression. "Well, he already knew. Coffey told him. He just wanted me to confirm it."

"Coffey told him we were sleeping together?"

Andie nodded. "They were like this—" she held her hand up, the first two fingers crossed "—when Dad was on the force. That's one of the main reasons I was so reluctant to call the police when all this started. I knew it would get back to my dad, and then I'd never hear the end of it." She shook her head. "He took it pretty good, though. I was surprised." Her father had asked a few questions, made a few suggestions and then pretty much dropped the subject, which was very unlike him.

Of course, now she knew why he'd taken it so well; he had a *man* to talk it over with and didn't think he needed to discuss it with her. "And here I thought, maybe, he was finally beginning to realize that I can look after myself."

"You're his daughter," Jim said, eyes downcast as he slipped his credit card into the back pocket of his jeans. "He's never going to realize you can take care of yourself, so you might as well resign yourself to it."

"TWO DAYS IS WAY TOO long," Jim groaned, dragging her into his arms as soon as they got inside the front door of her house. He kicked the door shut and tugged her T-shirt out of the waistband of her jeans, pushing it up so he could get at her breasts. "I've had a hard-on since we left Moose Lake, just thinking about getting you naked again, and then you make it worse by rubbing these—" he cupped her breasts in his hands "—against my back and running your hands all over my... Lord, Andrea, show a little mercy," he pleaded as she placed one hand on the straining front of his fly and squeezed.

"I thought that's what I was doing." She caressed him through his jeans. "Showing mercy."

"Ah, baby, you're killing me."

She started to draw her hand away, teasingly.

He reached down and pressed it more firmly against him. "Don't stop. Don't you dare stop. Not after teasing me for the past twenty miles."

"Didn't you like it?" she asked coyly, already knowing the answer, but needing to hear him say it, anyway.

"I loved it." He groaned as she popped open the

metal buttons on his fly and slipped her hands inside to caress his hard, bare flesh. "I love you."

He was too far gone to realize that she hadn't bridled or shied away from his declaration. Too deeply enmeshed in her sensual spell to be aware of anything beyond the purely physical. He shuddered as she stroked him, shivering uncontrollably. His breath rasped in and out of his lungs. His heart thudded against the wall of his chest.

Andie felt it all. The trembling muscles, the labored breathing, the frantic beating of his heart, the deep groans that he couldn't suppress. It made her feel powerful. Womanly. Giving. Greedy. She sank to her knees, dragging his jeans and briefs down with her, and took him in her mouth.

"Andrea." He moaned like a man mortally wounded, and fell back against the wall for support. "Oh, Andrea."

He reached down, cupping her head in his hands. His fingers curved around her skull, holding her as if she were made of the most delicate, most costly, most fragile glass imaginable. His eyes were nearly gold, glazed with passion and love as he watched her.

He'd had women on their knees in front of him before, but none of them had ever made him feel the way this woman made him feel. Proud. Humble. Grateful. Needy. His whole being was flooded with a terrible, aching tenderness and a burning need to give everything he was to her. To shelter and protect, to dominate, to own, to worship and adore the woman who was making him feel like a conquering hero. He wanted to lay his heart at her feet, to offer up his body to her service, to do great things in her honor. But she left him so weak, he could barely utter a word. And that word was her name.

"Andrea." He slid his hands from her head to her shoulders, grasping them to bring her to her feet and into his arms. "Andrea."

His mouth covered hers, open and seeking, devouring her in a kiss that was rapacious and adoring, savage and tender, sacred and profane all at once. Andie melted into his embrace, losing herself in the strength of his arms and the heat of his kiss, wanting what he wanted, willing, at that moment, to do or be or become whatever would please him most. She felt no fear at this loss of self, no anxiety, just an overwhelming need to give. Everything. She was completely open. Completely vulnerable. Completely at the mercy of the man who held her in his arms, kissing her as if he would never let her go, as if he would be content to continue kissing her, just kissing her, and nothing else, for the rest of forever.

And then the phone rang. Two shrill, strident blasts rent the air, piercing through the fevered stillness like gunshots through a peaceful forest.

Andie stiffened in his arms.

"Ignore it," Jim murmured, his voice guttural with need. "Just ignore it."

But the answering machine picked up and another voice began to fill the air.

"Whore," the voice said in a hoarse, angry whisper. "Faithless whore. Jezebel. I warned you, Bitch. I warned you. Now you'll pay."

12

JIM DREW BACK and looked down at her. Her stiffness, coupled with the flash of guilt in her eyes, told him this wasn't the first time she'd received a call like this. He put her away from him, very carefully, and reached down, yanking up his briefs and jeans, buttoning the fly as he strode toward the kitchen. Andie nervously smoothed her T-shirt down and followed him. The voice on the answering machine continued spewing out filth, growing louder and louder with each word.

Jim grabbed the phone off the hook. "Who is this?"

Silence.

"Who the hell is this?"

A dial tone was his only answer.

Deprived of the real target of his anger, he slammed the receiver down and turned on the only other person in the room. "How long has this been going on?"

"It hasn't." She came forward, her hand outstretched placatingly, frightened by the phone call—and by the look on his face. "Not like that."

"Not like that, how?"

"He hasn't screamed like that before, ever. His voice has always been calm and almost...*detached* is the only word I can think of. And up until a few days ago the calls were just..." She spread her hands. "They were annoying, but harmless. I didn't even connect them with what was going on at work, not until last Thurs—"

"Months? This has been going on for months and you haven't done anything about it? You haven't reported it to the police?"

"What could the police do for me, besides bring my father down on my head and complicate my life more than it already is? They'd have told me to change my telephone number and keep my doors locked. Well, I can't change my telephone number because of a few crank calls. I depend on it for my business. And I already have good sturdy locks on all my doors and windows. I know, I installed them myself and they're the best on the market."

"These are more than just a few crank calls, Andrea. Haven't you been listening? This guy is sick."

She shook her head. "They were just crank calls until last Thursday," she insisted. "There was nothing sexual about them before, at all. No overt threats. And he didn't start calling me names like that—" she gestured at the silent answering machine "—until then."

"The day after I started work for you. After the chandelier was broken."

"Yes," she said, although he hadn't really asked a question.

"After we started sleeping together."

"Yes."

"Why didn't you tell me?"

"Because at first, like I said, I didn't think they were connected with what's going on at the job site." She gripped her hands together on the kitchen counter. "And then, well..."

She'd wanted to tell him. Oh, how she'd wanted to tell him! She'd wanted to lay her fears and problems at his feet and let him solve them for her. So she hadn't.

Couldn't. It would have meant giving up control of her life, turning back into the same spineless, helpless, pitiful excuse for a human being she'd been nine years ago when anything beyond picking out new fabric for the kitchen curtains had been beyond her.

"I didn't tell you because it was—*is*—my problem, and I'd already taken what I felt was the next appropriate step to handle it."

"Your problem. I see." His voice was quiet, almost mild. If she'd known him better she'd have realized he only sounded that way when he was trying very hard not to lose his temper. "What next step?"

"I'm getting caller ID installed on Monday and an ala—"

"Caller ID? You think *caller ID* is going take care of this?"

"The phone company thought it was the best solution. I'll be able to capture the phone number the calls are coming from and I'd have something concrete to take to the poli—"

She jumped as his hand crashed down on the kitchen counter.

"My God, Andrea, are you out of your mind? Do you have any idea how serious this is? Any idea at all? This guy isn't just pissed off because you beat him out of a job. Not anymore. It's personal now. Hell, it's probably always been personal! You've just never given him any reason for jealousy before. But now you have. You've slept with me, and now he thinks you've betrayed him. This guy is obsessed with you, Andrea. Do you understand what an obsession is?" Jim grabbed her by the shoulders and shook her once, hard, feeling close to obsession himself. "Do you? Do you have any idea what this guy could do to you? My God, do you actually think caller ID and a couple of locks are going to be any help at all if he decides to come after you?"

"I'm not stupid," Andrea said, struggling to maintain her dignity—and her resolve—in the face of his fury and her own fear.

"Damn it, I didn't say you were stupid, I—"

"I'm not a child, either. I'm a grown woman who's looked at the situation from every angle and taken reasonable precautions to ensure my own safety."

"Reasonable? Do you actually call the way you're acting reasonable?"

"Yes, reasonable! And if you'd let me finish talking before you jump down my throat, you'd know I'm getting an alarm system installed, as well as caller ID," she said furiously. "What else would you have me do? Get a gun?"

"A gun!" The grisly statistics of crime victims killed with their own guns raced through his mind. "That's all you need. A damn gun in the house!"

"Then what else do you expect me to do?" She all but screamed the words at him. *"What?"*

"I expect you to call the police, and then pack a bag and go back up to your father's until they catch this guy."

"No." She tried to wrench her shoulders from his hands and was furious when she couldn't. "I'm not running away and letting someone else solve my problems for me," she said, glaring at him. "Would you expect a man to run away? Would *you* run away?"

"You're not a man, dammit! You're a woman. Look at you. The top of your head barely reaches my chin and you've got bones like a bird. You can't even get away from me, and I'm not holding you with near the force some deranged psychopath would, because I don't want to hurt you."

"Well, you *are* hurting me." She began twisting in his grasp, lifting her hands to push at his chest. It was like pushing against a brick wall. *"Let go!"*

He pulled her close, wrapping her in his arms instead. "Andrea, stop it. Stop it, now. Come on, baby, please." He tightened his arms, further restricting her movements, cradling her against him like one would a frantic child. "Stop it before you hurt yourself."

She stopped fighting suddenly, but didn't relax. Her body was still stiff, her muscles rigid and straining against him. "You can let me go now. Please," she added, when he didn't immediately loosen his hold. "I'm not hysterical. And I'm not going to get hysterical. I just want you to let me go."

He released her reluctantly, by degrees, his hands sliding from her back to her shoulders and down her arms as he stepped away from her. He took her hands in his and she let him have them without protest. They were limp and unresponsive.

"I'm just trying to help you, sweetheart." He raised each hand in turn and placed a kiss in the palm. "Why won't you let me help you?"

Andie steeled herself against the treacherous weakness that threatened to overwhelm her. It would be so easy to let him take care of her, to let him handle everything, to just turn her life over to him and go back to being what she had been before. So easy. There was only one way to protect herself and make sure it didn't happen, and that was to fight him—and herself, if need be—tooth and nail.

"I don't need your help," she said without looking at him. "I don't need it and I don't want it."

Jim couldn't believe it. Here he was, with his heart wide-open and his ego exposed, offering to put his body between her and whatever danger threatened her, and she'd thrown it all back in his face as if it didn't matter. As if *he* didn't matter to her at all. Like steel cable under too much pressure for much too long, his control finally snapped.

"Well, that's just too damn bad, isn't it?" he shouted. "Because you need my help, baby, and you've got it whether you want it or not." He thrust her hands away from him in disgust. "So deal with it."

"I don't have to deal with it," she shouted back. "In fact, I don't have to deal with you at all. You're fired."

"You can't fire me without cause. I'll file a grievance with the union."

"You're still on probation, remember? I can fire you for any reason I please, or no reason at all except that I think you're being a macho jerk." She raised her arm and pointed toward the door. "Get out of my house."

He crossed his arms and leaned back against the kitchen counter.

"I mean it," she said. "I want you to leave."

"So call a cop," he sneered.

"Don't think I won't."

"And admit you need help?" He shook his head. "I don't think so."

"I will," she threatened, but he'd already called her bluff and she knew it.

All she could do was simmer. She couldn't make him leave. She couldn't physically throw him out. She couldn't, when it came right down to it, make him do anything he didn't want to do. Not by herself. It made her absolutely furious.

"You're a bully, do you know that?" she fumed. "All men are bullies. Oh, some of you are more polished than others, and some of you hide it better, but deep down, you're all bullies and control freaks. If you can't make a woman do what you want by charming her into it or shaming her into it, you use tricks or threats or force. But you always get what you want, don't you? You always get your own way. Well, not this time. This time I'm going to have things *my* way."

She whirled away from him and reached for the phone. "Much as I hate to admit I need help, I'm going to call the police and have them haul you out of here by the scruff of your neck, if they have to. We'll see how smug you feel after they slap a pair of handcuffs on you."

"I don't think so." Jim reached out and took the receiver from her hand with an ease that further infuriated her. He put it back into the cradle. "Your father wouldn't like it."

"My father? What does my father have to do with this?"

Jim cocked a taunting eyebrow at her.

And suddenly, several seemingly unrelated incidents clicked into place. Bits of conversation mostly, things she hadn't really paid attention to on a conscious level; tiny hesitations and slips of the tongue that revealed more than was intended. Little facts Jim shouldn't have known, but did.

There's this great little hamburger place out on Excelsior... You probably pass right by it on your way home. How had he known where she lived?

Perp...contaminating the crime scene...dusting for finger-prints. Only one kind of person threw those phrases around so easily.

And he'd called her Andrea from the first, when no one outside of her family called her anything but Andie, anymore...including Dave Carlisle, the man who'd ostensibly sent Jim over to inquire about a job.

And that young female officer on Friday—hadn't she seemed a little confused about exactly who she was delivering her report to?

And hadn't Detective Coffey been just a bit too deferential? A little bit too ready to listen to a civilian's opinions? A bit too willing to let a potentially damning bit of evidence, like a bloody bandanna, be whisked aside without even a question?

And her father!

Her father's uncharacteristic lack of concern over the way she was handling the vandalism at the job site didn't mean he'd finally realized she could take care of herself. Oh, no, it meant he'd, once again, gone ahead and taken care of things for her. No wonder that conversation on the back porch hadn't been about Jim's "intentions." Her dad had been too busy listening to a firsthand crime report from a fellow professional to worry about the man's intentions toward his daughter.

Betrayal sliced through her, sharp and painful. Jim's. Her father's. She'd been manipulated, her wishes disregarded as if she were a child who didn't know what was good for her. She wondered if Natalie had known, too, that day—was it only last week?—when she'd advised Andie to take a lover, and indicated that the heartbreaker standing in the doorway at Belmont House would be a good candidate.

"You're a cop," she said flatly.

Jim nodded. "Detective Jim Nicolosi, currently on extended medical leave from the Minneapolis P.D., at your service."

"And my father hired you to be my baby-sitter, didn't he?"

"Bodyguard," Jim corrected. "And he didn't hire me, he asked me, as a former fellow officer, to do him a favor. And I agreed."

Andie waved the explanation away; explanations didn't matter because the result was the same. Treachery was treachery, no matter what the supposed justification. She'd been so proud of how far she'd come, proud of how she was handling her life. She thought she'd overcome the old dependency and powerlessness; she'd thought she was in charge and in control. What a joke that was! It seemed she was destined to always have some man in the background, pulling her strings.

"You lied to me."

"No, I didn't. Not once. Every word was the absolute truth." It just hadn't been the whole truth.

"You weaseled your way into a job with me under false pretenses. What's that if not lying?"

"What false pretenses? I *am* a finish carpenter. And a damn good one, too. I paid my way through college working summers in construction for my uncle, just like I said."

"And your so-called accident?"

"There's nothing 'so-called' about it. You've seen the scars." He touched his hip. "I went over the railing of a second-story fire escape while trying to cuff a scumbag crack dealer who'd just beaten the shit out of his girlfriend. I spent two months flat on my back because of it. And I'm still not a hundred percent." Jim hesitated, and then gave her something he'd never given anyone else, in penance for withholding the whole truth from her. "I may never be a hundred percent, physically or—" he swallowed, then forced himself to say it "—or psychologically. That's why I'm still on medical leave."

She had the grace to look shamefaced. "I'm sorry," she murmured, remembering what he'd said about his "little problem" with heights. "I didn't mean to belittle what happened to you."

"It's all right. You didn't know."

"No." Her gaze was unwavering, her expression faintly accusing. "I didn't know."

"Well, you know now," he blustered, feeling just a little bit guilty under the force of that steady look. "So..." he spread his hands. "Do you have any more questions? Is there anything else you'd like to know?"

"No," she said softly. "No more questions."

He reached out to take her in his arms. "Then come here."

She backed away quickly, astonished—and alarmed—that he could think the whole problem had been solved by his admission. "No."

"I love you, Andrea," he said. "And that's the absolute truth, too. I wish you'd believe it."

She looked up at him then, her eyes full of unshed tears. "You love who you think I am. Or who you want me to be. But I'm not her. I'm not some mindless little doll you can manipulate and control." Her hands curled into fists at her sides. "I'm *not*."

"I don't think of you as a doll, Andrea. I'm not in love

with a doll. I'm in love with you, exactly the way you are."

"How can you love me? You don't even know who I am."

"That's bull. I know exactly who you are. I've known exactly who you are from the very beginning."

"You only think you do," she said sadly, softly.

"Dammit, Andrea," he fumed, baffled by her insistence that he didn't know her, frustrated and frightened by her sudden apathy. He found himself wishing she'd yell at him again. She was too calm. Too...distant. It scared him. "You're not making any sense."

"No, probably not," she agreed listlessly, suddenly weary of trying to make him understand. "I'm tired. And upset. And I'd like you to leave now."

"I can't do that."

She looked up at him with a spark of her usual fire in her eyes. "Can't?"

"I'm not leaving you alone. Not with that creep—" he nodded at the phone "—still out there somewhere."

"I appreciate your concern. I really do. I'll lock my doors after you leave."

"You'll lock your doors," he agreed. "But we'll both be on this side of them." He reached out and took her clenched fists in his palms, cupping them. She stiffened but didn't back away. He could feel her trembling, see the pulse beating frantically in the hollow of her throat, and decided to try one more time. "I love you, Andrea. And what's more, you love me."

Speechless, Andie could only shake her head.

"Yes," he insisted softly. "You love me and, eventually..." he rubbed his thumbs back and forth across her knuckles, soothingly, and took the plunge "...eventually, you're going to marry me."

"No." Panic unlocked her vocal cords. She yanked her hands out of his. "No. I'm not marrying you. I'm never marrying anybody. Not ever again. Can't you understand? I don't want you here."

She didn't trust herself with him here. Even now, all she wanted to do was lay her head on his broad chest and let him take care of her for the rest of her life. If she let him stay, she might give in to the temptation to do just that and then she'd be lost again. Forever, this time.

"I don't want you anywhere near me," she said fiercely, when he just stood there, staring at her.

Her words cut soul-deep, hurting him more than he'd ever thought it was possible for anything to hurt. If he'd been a different man, a lesser man, he would have turned, then, and walked out of her life, leaving her safely barricaded behind the walls she'd erected. Except that she wasn't safe, not any longer, and it was his job to protect her.

"Tough," he said, hiding his pain behind a sneer. A man had his pride. "I'm here and I'm staying."

"If you won't leave, then I will," she threatened.

"I'll be right behind you. I'm not kidding, Andrea. I'm not letting you out of my sight until this creep is caught. If you really can't stand having me around, then I'll take you to your father's and you can stay there. Otherwise, consider us joined at the hip."

"And what I want doesn't matter?"

"No. In this case, it doesn't matter."

"I see." She was quiet a minute, absorbing that. "Am I allowed to go to my sister's alone? Or am I under house arrest?"

"If you want to visit your sister and her family, or your brother, or any of your friends, that's fine. I'll take you over, and I'll pick you up when you're ready to leave."

She nodded. "I don't need to be taken anywhere. I'm going to spend the night at Natalie's, and I'm driving myself. I'll go straight over. I won't stop or talk to strangers. You can follow me if you really feel you have to, but I'd rather you didn't."

"ANDREA! This is a pleasant surprise." Natalie pushed open the screen door. "Come on in. You're just in time to help me decide whether to have chocolate-chip mint or mocha fudge for dinner. Lucas and Ben—" Ben was their four-year-old son "—are having a boys' night out at McDonalds and I'm about to drive my..." She glanced over her sister's shoulder as she spoke, her attention caught by a movement in the driveway, and saw a hulking man in a leather jacket and a gleaming black helmet, straddling a rumbling Harley. "Who's that?" Her eyes widened in recognition and surprised delight when he pushed the visor of the helmet up. "My goodness. Did you actually take my advice?"

"Much to my everlasting regret," Andie said, and stepped inside her sister's house, slamming the door behind her.

"Andrea! How rude. Isn't he going to come in?"

"No."

"But, Andrea..." Natalie looked out over the top of the café curtain on her living-room window. "Are you just going to leave him sitting out there?"

"Until he rots," she snapped. "Or until he gets tired of waiting and goes home. I don't really care which."

"Well, he seems to be leaving." Natalie waved, as if sending an invited guest on his way, and then turned back to her sister, her brown eyes wide and interested. "What's going on?"

"Then you don't know?"

"Don't know what?"

"Oh, thank goodness. I thought... I was afraid..." Andie sank down on the plush, canvas-covered sofa in her sister's living room and started to cry.

"Andrea, honey." Natalie sat down beside her, the man on the motorcycle forgotten, and took her sister into her arms. "What's the matter?"

Andie told her. Everything. How she'd been manipulated and maneuvered by a man who professed to love her. How her wants had been ignored and ridden over roughshod. How she'd been tricked and mistreated by the very people she should have been able to trust.

"Men!" Natalie said, when Andie had finished. "I swear, sometimes I think we ought to just shoot them all and save ourselves the constant aggravation. Starting with that interfering old goat up at Moose Lake." She flashed a teasing, sideways glance at her sister. "Except then who would we get to kill the spiders for us?"

"I can kill my own spiders, thank you very much," Andie said, unwilling to be teased out of her resentment against the male of the species. "And so can you."

"Yeah, but it's so much more fun to let them do it for us. And it gives them something to get all manly and macho about. They need that outlet now and then, you know. Otherwise, they'd develop testosterone poisoning."

Andie gave a watery chuckle.

"Feel better now?"

Andie nodded.

"Crying jag over?"

"Yes."

"Good. Now let's talk about what's really bothering you."

"I *told* you what's bothering me."

"I don't think so." Natalie reached out and tucked a strand of hair behind Andie's ear. "Are you in love with him?"

She wanted to deny it. Oh, how she wanted to deny it. It would be so much easier if she could deny it. "Yes, dammit! Yes, I'm in love with him."

Natalie laughed. "I'm sorry," she said when her sister glared at her. "It's just that you looked so fierce and so...so disgusted with the whole thing."

"I am disgusted. With myself, mostly. I didn't mean to fall in love with him, Nat. I didn't mean to fall in love with anyone, ever again."

"Honey, falling in love isn't something to be afraid of. It's something to be celebrated and enjoyed and cherished for the miracle it is."

"For you, maybe. You're so strong and sure of yourself. You always have been. You didn't lose yourself when you married Lucas. He's got a forceful personality—"

"That's certainly putting it tactfully." Her husband was a steamroller.

"—But you didn't give up who you were and let him take over your life. I've always wondered how you did that."

"Honey, I was almost twenty-eight when I married Lucas. I'd been all grown up and on my own for years.

You were eighteen when you married Kevin. He was what? Twenty-four? And already the most arrogant, self-satisfied chauvinist pig it's ever been my misfortune to meet. It's amazing you stood up to him as well as you did."

"But I didn't stand up to him. I never stood up to him. I did everything he wanted. Everything. I let him run my life completely. I was a doormat, Natalie. A total doormat. And you know it."

"Well..." Natalie shrugged, but didn't disagree. "You're not a doormat anymore."

"Oh, but I am," Andie said quietly, as if admitting to some deep, dark perversion. "Deep down inside, I am. Don't you see? I *want* to let Jim handle this whole mess. I want to lay my head on his chest and have him put his arms around me and make it all go away."

"Well, what's wrong with that? We all want that sometimes. That doesn't mean you're a doormat."

"It's the first step to becoming one. If I let him handle this for me, then I'll let him handle something else. And pretty soon, I'll lift my head up off of his chest and realize he's taken over everything and my life won't be my own anymore."

"Has he actually tried to take over? Has he done or said anything that could be constituted as controlling in any way?"

"He followed me here, didn't he? He wouldn't leave my house when I told him to. He insisted that he was going to protect me whether I wanted him to or not."

Natalie snorted. "He's a cop, Andrea. And a man in love. Being overly protective is encoded in his DNA. So he followed you over here, so what? He's doing what he sees as his job. The real question is, did he try to stop you from coming in the first place?"

"Well...no."

"Has he tried to stop you from doing or saying anything you wanted to? Has he tried to make you do anything you *didn't* want to do? Has he belittled you or tried to make you feel stupid or—"

"He said I was out of my mind."

"Um-hmm. And what did you say to him?"

"I called him a macho jerk," she admitted.

"So you're even, then."

Andie shrugged.

"So, as I see it, Jim Nicolosi is just a your average macho-type guy, given to occasional chest beating and thick-headedness, but all in all, nice to have around." Natalie's eyes sparkled mischievously, inviting her sister to smile. "Not to mention gorgeous to look at and, apparently, great in the sack, too."

Andie missed the gleam in her sister's eyes completely. "There's nothing average about him," she said, leaping to his defense as if her sister had just maligned him instead of complimenting him. "Nothing. He's incredibly...sweet, actually. And sexy. And he makes me feel sexy, too. And beautiful."

"Then what's the problem?"

"Me," Andie said. "I'm the problem."

13

"SHE ACCUSED ME of lying. Lying! Me! She said I was a control freak and that I was trying to manipulate her."

Jim's three sisters looked at each other over the long trestle table in Janet's cozy colonial-style kitchen, watching their only brother push strawberry shortcake around on his plate while he ranted on about how a woman named Andrea Wagner was driving him absolutely crazy. Sunday dinner was long over and they'd been sitting there for twenty minutes over second cups of cooling coffee while their respective husbands and children frolicked outside in the pool.

Janet raised her elegant eyebrows over his last comment.

Jessie rolled her eyes.

Julie laughed out loud.

Jim glared at them over the rim of his coffee cup. "What the hell's so funny?"

"Jimmy, honey, I hate to side with the, uh, enemy here," Janet said, shushing the more plainspoken Julie with a single admonishing look. "But you *are* a control freak."

He turned his glare on his oldest sister. She stared steadily back, as unimpressed by his scowl as his other two sisters. He set his coffee mug down on the wooden table with a sharp little click.

"No other woman has ever accused me of trying to run her life," he said indignantly.

"Probably because none of the other women you've ever dated have been smart enough to realize you were doing it," Julie said bluntly. She'd always been unimpressed by and outspoken regarding the caliber of women her brother dated.

"Doing *what*, dammit? What do I do?"

"You roll over 'em like a Sherman tank," Julie said. "You mow 'em down—" she made a swooping gesture with her hand, accompanied by a noise meant to imitate a fast, low-flying airplane "—anytime they dare to have an opinion contrary to yours."

"That's a slight exaggeration." Jessie, the lawyer, swatted her younger sister on the arm. "He doesn't usually have to roll over them because most women are so bowled over by his pretty face—" she patted his cheek "—that they fall all over themselves to do what he wants, almost before he knows what that is."

Jim ducked away from her hand. "Now you're exaggerating."

"No, she's not," Janet said. "Most of the women you've dated up to now—"

"All," Julie interrupted.

"Most," Janet said firmly. "Most of the women you've dated have been the compliant type."

"That means they didn't mind when you bossed them around," Julie informed him.

"Because of that pretty face," Jessie added.

He ignored both of them. "And the ones that weren't compliant?"

"You didn't notice and they finally just drifted away.

Like Michele," Janet said, mentioning the girl he'd almost been engaged to in his twenties.

"Michele and I wanted different things."

"And you didn't care enough to try to find a compromise that worked for both of you," Janet said.

"Well, neither did she," he said defensively. "What does that have to do with now?"

"What it has to do with now, pea brain," Julie said, "is that Michele was an independent woman with a mind and opinions of her own. Apparently, so is this woman you're involved with now. And independent women don't appreciate it when some man tries to tell them how to run their lives. Especially women with controlling ex-husbands in their backgrounds."

"But I'm not trying to tell her how to run her life, dammit, I'm trying to protect her!"

"Maybe she doesn't want your protection. Have you thought of that?"

"She doesn't know what she wants right now. She's under a lot of pressure and she's upset, so she isn't thinking straight. Otherwise, she'd admit I'm right."

The three women looked at each other, then at him, and shook their heads sadly.

"I hope you didn't say that to her," Janet said.

"Oh, you know he did," Jessie said. "Otherwise, he wouldn't be over here bellyaching to us about the sorry shape his love life's in."

"Should I explain it to him?" Julie asked. "Or would one of you like to do the honors?"

Both her sisters conceded the floor to her.

"Look, Jim, we know you think you're doing the right thing because you always do—think you're doing the right thing, I mean. But you've got to back off and give this woman a little room or you're going to lose her, just like you lost Michele."

"I didn't lose Michele. We made a mutual decision to stop seeing each other."

"Well, it sounds to me like Andrea Wagner has made a unilateral decision to stop seeing you."

"When this is over and she's had a chance to calm down and think about it, she'll change her mind." *I'll see to it*, he promised himself.

"Not if you keep pushing her, she won't," Jessie snapped, her voice rife with affectionate exasperation. "From what you've told us, I'd say she's had it up to here—" she drew her hand across her forehead "—with condescending, patronizing men who think they know what's best for her. And, as well-meaning as some of those men might be, she's bound to resent it. I know I would." She looked around at her sisters. "Any of us would."

Well-meaning. The word rang a warning bell in his mind. Hadn't Andie already condemned him once for his "well-meaning interference"? And hadn't she accused him of patronizing her, too?

Did that mean his sisters were right?

Was he really in danger of losing her?

"We know you're head over heels in love with her, Jimmy," Janet said, her tone more kindly and understanding than that of her sisters. "That's as plain as the nose on your handsome face. But don't you think you might be overreacting because of that? Maybe this whole thing isn't as serious as you think it is."

"No." Jim shook his head. On this one point, he was absolutely sure. "She needs protection whether she knows it or not. She's being *stalked*, dammit."

"Well, does it have to be you, then?"

"What do you mean, does it have to be me? Of course it has to be me. She's my woman. My responsibility."

"Oh, brother!" Jessie rolled her eyes again. "Do you realize how arrogant that sounds?"

"Arrogant? What's arrogant about it? It's the plain truth. She's my woman and I'm going to protect her, whether she wants to be protected or not."

If he lost her because of that, well, then he lost her. Her safety came first. But he didn't plan on losing her.

"She's her *own* woman, you moron." Julie pushed back her chair and stood up so she could stare down at him. "An adult who's perfectly capable of making her own decisions about whether she needs protection or not."

"And what if she makes the wrong decision?"

"It's still *her* decision."

Jim stood, too. "No, it's—"

"That's enough, you two." Janet clapped her hands together, reprimanding them the way she did her children. "Just stop it right now and sit down, both of you."

With one final glare at each other, they sat.

"I know you'll do what you think you have to do, no matter what anyone says," Janet said to her brother. "But think about this for a minute.... You say she needs protection. Fine, maybe she does. It's part of your job to know those things, so I won't argue with you about that. But should that person really be you?" She held up her hand when he would have spoken. "No, don't look at me like that. I'm not suggesting you *can't* protect her. Medical leave or not, we all know you can. But you said she's already taken several steps to protect herself. She's got good locks on her house. She's installing caller

ID and an alarm system. She's notified the police and alarmed the job site. It sounds to me as if she's a reasonable woman—"

Reasonable. That's just what Andrea had said. Did that mean she, and his sisters, were right? Did that mean *he* was being unreasonable?

"—taking reasonable precautions under the circumstances. If you really think she needs a bodyguard, why don't you suggest...*suggest,*" she emphasized, "that she hire one of her own choosing? That way, she'll have the protection you think she needs, it'll be her decision and you won't be put in the position of telling her what to do."

"And if she won't hire someone?"

"Then, like Julie said, that's her decision. And she'll have to live with it."

"Or not live with it," Jim said. "And *I* couldn't live with that."

CONVINCED BY HIS SISTERS that some kind of compromise was called for if he didn't want to lose Andrea, Jim called Natalie's. Andie wasn't there.

"She left about thirty minutes ago," Natalie said. "She said she was going home."

"And you just let her go?"

"My sister's a grown woman," Natalie informed him. "She didn't ask my permission."

"Grown woman or not, you should have stopped her."

"And just how would you suggest I might have done that?" Natalie snapped. "She wasn't in any mood to listen to reason. What was I supposed to do, tie her up?"

"If that's what it took," Jim growled, and hung up on her.

His first instinct was to drive straight over to Andrea's house to make sure she was all right—and then yell at her for disobeying him. His sisters encouraged him to call her first.

"Don't tell her you're coming over. *Ask*," they said.

But she didn't answer her phone. Not even when he identified himself on her answering machine.

"Dammit, dammit, dammit," Jim berated himself. "I knew I shouldn't have left her alone. Dammit, I *knew* it!"

"It doesn't have to mean anything sinister," Jessie said.

"No, of course it doesn't," Julie agreed. "She probably just doesn't want to talk to you, is all, so she's not picking up."

"Then why wouldn't she just unplug the phone?"

"She's got kids," Janet explained. "She wouldn't do that in case they called."

Jim held on to his growing sense of panic and called her one more time. "If you're there, Andrea, pick up. Otherwise, I'm coming over."

There was still no answer.

She might not be there at all.

Or she be there and was stubbornly refusing to answer the phone.

Or she might be there and *unable* to answer the phone.

He slammed the receiver down and rushed out of his sister's house, intent on finding out for sure.

But when he got to Andie's house, no one was home. He forced himself to go inside and look around to make absolutely sure of that, to check for signs of a break-in or a struggle. From the outside, the house was exactly the same as they'd left it when she'd locked up to go to her sister's.

"All right, Andrea," he murmured to himself. "Where are you? Where would you go?"

There was only one answer.

Belmont House.

ANDIE HAD INTENDED to go home when she left Natalie's, she really had, but the thought of being alone was unsettling. It wasn't that she was scared, exactly. She was just restless, and she knew she'd end up wandering from room to room, looking for something—anything—to keep her busy, just the way she had after Chris and Emily had left for Moose Lake with their grandfather and Kyle had flown off to California.

She'd fixed every leaky faucet in the house during that first lonely week by herself. She'd planed and rehung a door that had been sticking for years. She'd painted the boys' rooms, repapered Emily's and installed a set of built-in bookshelves on either side of the fireplace in the family room in an effort to fill up the empty spaces her children had left.

Now it appeared there was another empty space—where Jim Nicolosi belonged. She hadn't looked for it. She hadn't wanted it. But there it was. She knew now that she'd been lying to herself. She was in love with him, probably had been from the beginning. But the trust...ah, the trust came harder. And it was *herself* she didn't trust, not him. Her talk with Natalie had made her realize that. Jim Nicolosi was a good man, eminently worthy of her love and trust. The question was

was she enough of a woman to give him what he needed? What he deserved? Could she untangle herself from the injustices of the past so that she could deal fairly with the future?

It was something she was going to have to figure out. And soon.

But now, right now, she needed action, something to keep her hands busy while her mind went round and round.

Without really thinking about it, she found herself driving to Belmont House.

The sun was just dipping below the trees along Lake of the Isles when she got there. Long, wavering shadows tinged with pink and gold skimmed over the water and between the lovely old houses, slowly melding into twilight. Andrea parked her battered pickup in the driveway and got out, automatically leaning back in to grab her tool belt and strap it on around her waist.

There was a No Trespassing sign on the front lawn and another tacked up on the front door. Neither had been disturbed. The house itself stood silent, seemingly inviolate. She fished her key ring out the pocket of her jeans and selected the appropriate two keys. Unlocking the door, she pushed it open and started to step inside.

"Nice evening, isn't it?" said a voice behind her.

Andie nearly jumped out of her skin.

"Oh, I'm so sorry. We didn't mean to frighten you," the owner of the voice said pleasantly.

"Mr. and Mrs. Hastings. How nice to see you. How have you—"

A low, warning buzz sounded.

"I don't mean to be rude, but could you hold on just

a minute?" Andrea said. "I have to punch in the code before the alarm goes off."

She stepped inside the door to the control panel and punched in a four-number code. The warning buzz died. The row of lights across the top of the panel blinked off, indicating that she'd successfully disarmed the system.

"There, that's better," she said as she came back out on the porch. "Now, how are you?"

"Oh, we're fine. Just fine," Mr. Hastings answered for them both. "Taking our evening constitutional. Good for the heart, you know."

"How are you, dear?" asked Mrs. Hastings, concern in her voice. "That was certainly a bad business the other day. Most distressing." She reached out and patted Andie's arm. "I just wish we could have been more help to that nice young police officer."

"The police interviewed you?" Andie said.

"Oh, my, yes." Mrs. Hastings faded blue eyes were aglow with the memory. "But I'm afraid we weren't much help at all, really. Neither one of us sees as well as we used to, more's the pity, and Mr. Hastings's hearing isn't what it once was. Of course, we were inside and asleep when it happened, so even if there had been something to see, we wouldn't have been out here to notice. I am so terribly sorry for that, dear. I do hope it doesn't mean the police have lost a valuable clue."

"Don't be. Please." Andie hid a smile, knowing the woman was as sorry for missing the action as she was for missing something that might be of help to the police. "The vandal broke in through a rear window, so you wouldn't have seen anything in any case, even if it hadn't happened in the dead of night."

"Well, that's comforting."

"Yes, isn't it?" Andrea agreed, wondering how best to send the two gregarious old people on their way so she could get to work. "I don't want to seem inhospitable, but I do have work to do, so..."

"You aren't actually intending to work in there alone, are you, dear?"

"Yes, I am."

"Oh dear. We know it's your habit to do so, of course." Mrs. Hastings glanced at her husband. "We've seen you from our porch many evenings," she admitted. "But do you think it's quite wise now, after what's happened?"

"I'm perfectly safe," Andie assured them. "You saw me disarm the alarm system. When I go inside I'll arm it again. No one will be able to get in without setting it off. And I guarantee—" she smiled at Mr. Hastings "—you'll be able to hear it all the way to the Mississippi River if it does."

"Then we'd best be letting you get to work. Come along, Ella." Mr. Hastings put his hand under his wife's elbow. "Good night, Miss Wagner."

Andie stood and watched them maneuver their way down the walk, then she stepped inside Belmont House, closed the door and set the alarm. It was eerily quiet. And empty. Full of dim, shadowy corners and those faint, creaky, creepy sounds that old houses make.

"Oh, don't be ridiculous," she chided herself, but she couldn't help but look over her shoulder as she headed upstairs through the darkened house.

She intended to finish dismantling the mahogany surround on the tub. She'd meant to do that on Friday, so they could start removing the old plumbing on Monday, but then all hell had broken loose and plans had changed. If she did it tonight, things could still progress pretty much on schedule.

She was kneeling on the floor, light from the battery-powered work lamp falling over her hands as she removed the mahogany panels that enclosed the tub, when she heard a noise downstairs. She stiffened, her fingers tightening around the screwdriver, her skin prickling in response, her ears straining *not* to hear it again.

Was that a footstep?

No, surely not!

There was no one here but her, and no one could get in without setting off the alarm.

She *had* set the alarm.

Hadn't she?

Yes. Yes, of course she had. The little row of lights had gone on, indicating that the system was armed.

The house was just settling around her, the way old houses did.

But it certainly sounded like a footstep.

Footsteps, plural.

Someone was coming up the stairs.

But that was impossible.

The alarm hadn't gone off.

It would have gone off if someone had tried to open a door or broken a window.

Unless you had the code, you couldn't get in.

Who else had the code?

"Dot," she murmured with relief.

Dot had the code. Andie had given it to her in case

she was ever delayed or otherwise unable to be there to open the doors for the crew.

And Jim, too.

Of course!

It was Jim.

It had to be.

With the screwdriver clutched in one hand, the work lamp in the other, she jumped up and hurried toward the door of the master bathroom, heading for the hallway and the grand staircase. She didn't stop to think about the sense of relief that flooded her, the sense of well-being, the sense of joy. She just rushed down the hall to meet him.

"Oh, Jim, I'm so glad you came. I have so much to tell you. So—"

It wasn't Jim.

She stopped at the top of the stairs, staring down at the man who was slowly climbing them.

"Pete?" she said uncertainly.

Did Pete have the code, too? She didn't remember giving it to him. But maybe Dot had. He might have needed to pick something up or drop something off, and so Dot had given him the code. Hiding her disappointment that it wasn't Jim, Andie smiled and started down the stairs.

"Pete, what are you doing here on a Sunday? At this time of night? It's—" she glanced at her watch, turning her wrist carefully so as not to stick herself with the screwdriver, and lifted the work lamp higher so she could read the face "—almost nine o'clock."

He looked up at her then, and the expression in his eyes chilled her to the bone. "I warned you," he said.

14

ANDIE DIDN'T TRY to reason with him. You couldn't reason with madness. She threw the lamp at him as hard as she could and ran, fleeing back up the stairs. In that split second before she took action, she thought of running downstairs past him, toward the front door. It was the closest exit. But he was a big man and he stood in the center of the staircase, and she didn't dare risk it. If he caught her, he would hurt her; it was there in his eyes.

She could hear him pounding up the steps behind her, his work boots thudding against the hardwood runners. She imagined she could feel his breath on the back of her neck, his hands reaching for her, touching her. Fear crawled up her spine, spurring her to move faster, and she ducked into one of the empty bedrooms, plastering herself against the wall, thanking God that she still wore her tennis shoes and not the heavy work boots that announced every footstep.

The tennis shoes gave her a slight advantage. All she had to do was wait, to conquer her fear and judge her moment. When he passed by the door, she could slip out behind him and run down the stairs to safety and freedom.

"There's nowhere you can hide that I won't find you, Andrea," he said as he came down the hall. "Nowhere you can run."

Andie pressed herself against the wall, the screwdriver clutched in her hand, and waited...waited for his shadow to pass the doorway. *Any minute now,* she told herself as she stood there, listening to his footsteps. *Any second.*

But he halted in front of the door instead.

"I know you're in there, Andrea. I can hear you breathing."

Andie sucked in her breath and held it.

He stepped into the room. "It's fitting, don't you think," he said conversationally, "that you should receive your punishment here, Andrea. If you'd stayed home like a good woman, if you'd followed your ordained role, I wouldn't have to do this."

Wait, she told herself, fighting panic. *Wait. Let him come farther into the room, then you can slip by.* She could just see him, there inside the doorway, his body a darker shadow than those surrounding him, blocking her only exit. *Wait.*

"I was only going to chastise you for your disobedience, Andrea. But you wouldn't listen to me. You wouldn't obey me."

Come on. Come on. Just one more step. That's it, she urged him silently. *That's it. Now another. Come on!*

"You betrayed me, instead. With him. You whored yourself." Pete paused and lifted his head, sniffing the air like an animal, then turned and headed in her direction. "And now you have to be punished. Severely punished. I warned you."

Andie shrank back, trying to make herself smaller, trying to disappear into the wall, willing him not to see her, to pass by.

His hand shot out, grabbing her arm.

She screamed and stabbed him with her screwdriver, driving it as hard as she could into his hand. She felt it hit bone.

"Bitch!" he roared, and let her go. "Wanton bitch!"

Andie ran. Faster than she had ever run in her life. Out of the room. Down the hall. Toward the grand staircase. She felt his fingers clutching at the back of her T-shirt, and she screamed again and stumbled forward, nearly losing her balance as her foot knocked against the work lamp and sent it rattling the rest of the way down the stairs. She was at the bottom, almost to the door, when he tackled her from behind. They went down in a tangled heap, rolling across the floor, Andie kicking and screaming, her fingers curled and going for his eyes. She felt the work lamp hit her in the back as they crashed against it. Felt Pete's hot breath in her face and his hands scrambling to find purchase and hold her still. She was breathing with heavy, panting gasps, half sobbing, half cursing, almost blinded by panic, her strength rapidly draining away as she tried to fight him off.

He was screaming as wildly as she, sick words and phrases, threats, incoherent pleas.

Then something connected—her nails or her knee, she didn't know which—and his grip loosened for just a moment. She scrambled away from him, crablike, trying to get to her feet before he recovered and came after her again.

He lunged forward, extending himself full length, and grabbed her ankle.

She kicked out, landed him a solid blow on his neck, and gained her release.

But he was still between her and the door, still between her and freedom. He was getting to his feet again, coming after her again. Andie picked up the work lamp and heaved it with all her strength—not at him, but at the long, stained-glass window by the door.

Some feral, unconscious part of her mind had noticed that the lights above the control panel were blinking. The alarm system was still on. All she had to do was set it off to bring the entire neighborhood to the door.

The lamp slammed against the window, shattering it, and the alarm went off, shrieking its warning into the warm summer night.

"Bitch!" he screamed again, as he threw himself at her. "Faithless, whoring bitch!"

Andie eluded him and began scrambling up the scaffolding.

JIM HEARD THE ALARM go off when he was still two blocks away. Two agonizingly long blocks away. He revved up the Harley and ran a red light, leaving drivers honking and cursing behind him. He could see Andie's truck as he rounded the corner, and the neighbors already coming out of their houses to see what all the commotion was about. He burned rubber as he brought the Harley to a stop behind her truck, laying it down on the pavement as he leaped from the saddle and ran toward the house.

"Minneapolis P.D.," he shouted as he ran. "Someone call 911. Tell them there's an assault in progress and an officer needs help. Do it!"

The front door was locked. He lifted his foot and kicked it in, crashing into the foyer. "Andrea!"

"Up here!"

He could barely hear her over the shrieking of the

alarm. Could barely see in the darkened room. "Where? Andrea, where are you?"

"Up here. Oh, thank God, Jim. I'm—"

He heard her scream clearly. It was bloodcurdling. Terrified. The scream of a woman in mortal fear for her life.

He looked up toward the sound. And up.

She was clinging to the scaffolding with both hands, half dangling over the topmost edge, kicking at the man who held her ankle in his grasp, trying to drag her off from the level below.

"Whore!" Peter Lindstrom screamed. "Faithless whore. He can't save you. Only I can save you."

Jim didn't even have to think about it. His fear of heights was nothing compared to his fear that he might lose Andie. He swung himself up onto the bottom rung of the scaffolding and started climbing. It took him only minutes to reach the maniac who held Andie captive. Jim grabbed him around the knees, jerking him off of his feet, using his own weight to break the man's grip on her ankle. They fell backward together, tumbling to the narrow boards that composed the second level of scaffolding. Only the crossed bars kept them from crashing to the floor.

Jim felt a bar slam against his back with a sickening thud, a grim reminder of what had happened when he'd broken through the rusted-out railing of the fire escape. But the bar held, and he held on, rolling back and forth in the small space, trying to gain the upper hand and subdue the berserk attacker.

As the two men pummeled each other and fought for dominance, the alarm cut off suddenly. In its place the sound of police sirens rent the air, growing louder and louder. Pete Lindstrom roared his defiance and reared up, yanking Jim with him, obviously intent on taking both of them over the edge. Jim caught one of the bars in the crook of his elbow and held on, curling his arm up, wrapping his fingers around the bar above it for better purchase and letting Pete think he was succeeding. They went over the side together. Jim was jerked back, anchored by the way his arm was wrapped around the bar. He slammed into the scaffolding, hitting it with enough force to rattle his teeth and set the whole structure trembling. Pete lost his grip and plunged to the floor. He landed with a thud at the feet of the police officers who burst in the front door.

"Oh, my God! Oh, my God! Jim." Andie scrambled down from the third level of scaffolding on her hands and knees, reaching out, grabbing Jim's shirt and his belt to help him crawl back up on the narrow boards of the second level. "Are you all right? Oh, my God. Your hip. Is it all right? It's all my fault." She was crying and kissing him at the same time, running her hands over him to check for damage. "All my fault. Are you all right?"

"Andrea, sweetheart. I'm fine." He was pretty sure he'd popped something important loose in his shoulder, but she didn't need to know that. He wrapped his good arm around her and pressed her close. "Are *you* all right? Did he hurt you?"

"No, he didn't hurt me. I'm fine." She wrapped her arms around him and held on for dear life. "Now that you're here, I'm fine."

THEY WERE SEPARATED at the hospital, Jim shunted off into one examining room and Andie into another.

Jim had dislocated his shoulder and had to have it popped back into place and wrapped, but, amazingly, there had been no damage done to his hip. And he'd decided his fear of heights was gone for good.

Andie suffered various scrapes and bruises, none of them serious enough to require bandaging, though she had a knot the size of a hen's egg where she'd rapped her head against the floor.

Pete Lindstrom had been taken immediately into emergency surgery.

"Nasty compound fracture of his left leg," said the police officer who sat waiting outside the green curtain while Andie had her scrapes and bruises attended to. "Some internal bleeding, too, but they've got that under control. The doc says it looks like he's going to make it."

"And then what happens to him?" Andie asked, when the nurse pushed aside the curtain and silently gave the police officer permission to begin taking her statement.

"The shrinks will get a hold of him next, then—" the officer shrugged and flipped open his notebook "—who knows? It'll depend on just how sick he is."

"I don't know why or how he became obsessed with me," Andie said, after she gave the officer all the facts she could. "I mean, I've known him for several years but I've never dated him or anything. You couldn't even have called us friends, really. He was too taciturn and withdrawn for that. We worked on a couple of the same jobs, early on in my career. And then, when I won the bid on Belmont House and needed more carpenters, he was one of those who applied for the job. But there was never the slightest *hint* that he had any kind of feeling for me. Never."

She kept shooting glances at the doorway as she spoke, expecting to see Jim at any moment. But he didn't come.

Where was he?

"Have you taken Jim's statement yet?" she asked, when the officer folded up his notebook.

"Jim?"

"Detective Nicolosi," she said. "The man they brought me in with?"

"Oh, no. Coffey's got him in the room next door. Hey, wait a minute," he said as Andie slid down off of the examining table. "Do you think you should be moving around by yourself? Aren't you supposed to be in a wheelchair or something?"

Andie ignored him and strode through the door, almost knocking down Jim, who was right outside *her* door.

"What are you doing loitering around out here?" she asked him. "Why didn't you come in?"

"I was giving you some space."

"Space? What do I need space for?"

He shrugged, then winced and glanced at his shoulder. "I thought you might, ah...need it after what happened and all."

"I'll let you know when I need space." She took hold of his good arm and steered him into the examining room she had just vacated. "Was there anything else, Officer?" she said to the man who still stood by the examining table.

"No, ma'am. I think that will do it for now."

"Then would you excuse us, please?"

"It's okay, Madison," Jim said when the officer hesitated. "She's unarmed."

Madison left and Andie maneuvered Jim back against the examining table. "Why are you avoiding me all of a sudden?"

"I'm not avoiding you. I'm trying to show a little sensitivity here, is all."

She narrowed her eyes at him. "I thought you loved me."

"I *do* love you! What the hell does that have to do with anything?"

"I needed you with me," she said. "I *wanted* you with me. Desperately. And you were off in some other room with Detective Coffey."

"Wait a minute." Jim held up the hand that wasn't strapped to his chest. "Just wait one minute. Aren't you the woman who said I was trying to control her life? Didn't you accuse me of bullying you and telling you what to do? Aren't you the very same woman who said you didn't need me or any other man?"

"Did I say that?"

He lowered his brows. "Andrea."

"All right. You're right. I said it. And I meant it at the time but..."

"But?"

"Well. I've had some time to think about it and... and I..." Why was it so hard to admit? Why couldn't she just come right out and say it? He deserved to hear her say it. "I was wrong," she said. "I do need you. It wasn't you I didn't trust to let me make my own decisions, it was me."

"You didn't trust yourself?"

"I was afraid if I let myself lean on you at all, afraid that if I did I'd turn back into the spineless wimp I used to be."

"You? Spineless? Sweetheart..." He reached out and cupped her face with his free hand. "You have the courage of a lion, don't you know that? There aren't many women who could do what you did tonight, let alone what you've been doing for the last nine years. Your courage is one of the things I love most about you."

She felt her eyes well up.

"That, and those pretty little breasts of yours," he growled.

Her eyes cleared as if by magic, which was what he intended.

She went up on tiptoe and pressed a quick kiss against his mouth, a silent thank-you for his understanding.

"I learned something important about myself tonight," Andie said. "I learned that I'm strong enough to cope with anything."

"Didn't I just tell you tha—"

Andie pressed her fingertips against his lips. "I also learned that even the strongest person needs someone to lean on, and it doesn't make me less my own person to need you. It doesn't take away any of my independence or autonomy to admit that. But most importantly—" she gazed up into his eyes "—I learned that I love you."

This time Jim's eyes filled, their brown lightening to purest gold. "Andrea—"

She didn't let him speak. "All the time I was up on that scaffolding, fighting for my life, the only thing I could think of was you. I didn't want to die before I could tell you how I felt."

"Andrea, sweetheart." He gathered her in his good

arm and held her tight, then bent his head and took her mouth in a long, sweet kiss.

A nurse popped into the room. "Oh, sorry," she said to the entwined couple, "I can use the other examining room. No problem." She popped out again.

Coffey poked his head in a minute later. "Anyone need a ride anywhere?" he asked. "Oh, guess not," he said, and withdrew.

"Umm," Andie sighed, when Jim finally released her lips. She wrapped her arms around his waist and rested her head on his uninjured shoulder for a moment. "Jim?" she murmured.

"What, sweetheart?" he said into her hair.

"Will you marry me?"

"*What?*"

She lifted her head to look at him. "Will you marry me?"

Jim started to laugh.

Andie thought she should probably be insulted, but it was nice laughter and he held her with his good arm while his chest rumbled against hers. "Would you like to tell me what's so funny?" she asked, when he got control of himself again.

"I feel just like Doris Day," he said.

Epilogue

Two years later

"COME ON, HURRY UP," Emily urged, practically dancing with impatience as she stood on the sidewalk outside of Belmont House. "We'll be late for the party. Everybody's inside already."

"You run on ahead then, sweetheart," Jim said to her as he extended both hands to help Andie out of the car. "I'll see that your mother gets there. It's going to take her a few minutes."

Emily hesitated. "Are you sure?"

"Go on," Andie said, as Jim pulled her to her feet. She emerged from the car belly first, heavily pregnant and looking as if she might go into labor at any minute. "You can scope me out a good seat. You two go with her," she said to her sons, seeing their impatience. "And take Grandpa's birthday present with you."

She stood in the open doorway of the car, one hand on her husband's arm and one on the door frame, watching her three children as they made their way across the brick walk and up the stairs into Belmont House. Kyle and Chris maneuvered their grandfather's bulky birthday gift between them—a fishing-pole rack they'd all had a hand in making—while Emily fluttered and fussed, offering advice and looking adorable in her sixties-inspired party dress.

They were good kids. Kids to be proud of.

Her sons were young men now, at eighteen and twenty years old, and handsome enough to have girls calling at all hours of the day and night. Her daughter had just turned fourteen and, miraculously, seemed to have avoided developing the typical teenage girl's disdain for her mother...so far. Now here Andie was forty years old, married again when she'd vowed it would never happen. And about to become a mother for the fourth time.

She knew she should feel like an idiot, pregnant at her age, but except for the nagging ache in her lower back and her swollen ankles, she'd never felt better—or happier—in her life. That feeling, she knew, was thanks to the man standing at her side.

They'd been married in Belmont House nearly two years ago, the first wedding held in the newly renovated landmark that had, indeed, made Andie's reputation as a contractor. She was much in demand now, able to wait for people to come to her instead of pounding the pavement looking for customers. If the public wanted to believe that her all-woman crew was more meticulous and detail oriented than an all-male crew would be, then so be it. That belief only added to her bottom line.

The fiasco with poor Pete Lindstrom had added to her bottom line, too, for a while. The story had made all the local papers and had been a nine days' wonder until the hearing that sent Pete to a mental institution for treatment. She'd heard he'd been released a few months ago and was now living quietly with his family in Wisconsin—where Jim had a police buddy who was discreetly keeping track of his movements, especially any that might bring him in the direction of Minneapolis.

"Everything okay?" Jim said, reaching down to put his hand on the hard curve of his wife's swollen belly.

She turned her head and smiled up at him. "Everything's wonderful," she said, covering his hand to hold it against her belly as she lifted her face for his kiss.

It was a lovers' kiss, deep and thorough and passionate, and it didn't end until the baby kicked against its parents' hands.

Jim smiled against his wife's lips. "We woke her up."

"She's a sucker for her father's charm, just like her mama." Andie patted her husband's hand and reluctantly drew away. "We'd better go in or Dad'll be coming out here to see what's keeping us."

They were celebrating her father's seventieth birthday today, almost two weeks early because Andie's due date was *on* his birthday and nobody wanted to take any chances on her delivering during the party. Nathan Bishop was fully expecting her to deliver on schedule, though, and Andie was sure he'd take it as another example of feminine perversity if she didn't.

"Surprise!" everyone yelled, as she and Jim came through the front door of Belmont House.

It wasn't a birthday party, it was a baby shower.

"Oh. Oh, my." Andie's eyes misted over, which surely wouldn't have happened but for the pregnancy hormones surging through her body. *"Oh!"*

"Andrea?" Jim stiffened in alarm at her sudden stillness. "What is it? Is it the baby? Are you all right?"

"My water just broke."

"Your water..." He looked down at the darkened streaks of dampness marring the front of her lavender maternity dress...down at her soaked shoes and the puddle on the floor between her feet, and then back up at her face. "But you're not due for two weeks."

"Surprise," she said. "Not even you can control this."

Pamela Burford presents

The Wedding Ring

*Four high school friends and a pact—
every girl gets her ideal mate by thirty or be
prepared for matchmaking! The rules are
simple. Give your "chosen" man three
months...and see what happens!*

Love's Funny That Way
Temptation #812—on sale December 2000
It's no joke when Raven Muldoon falls in love with comedy
club owner Hunter—*brother* of her "intended."

I Do, But Here's the Catch
Temptation #816—on sale January 2001
Charli Ross is more than willing to give up her status as
last of a dying breed—the thirty-year-old virgin—to Grant.
But all *he* wants is marriage.

One Eager Bride To Go
Temptation #820—on sale February 2001
Sunny Bleecker is still waiting tables at Wafflemania when
Kirk comes home from California and wants to marry her.
It's as if all her dreams have finally come true—except...

Fiancé for Hire
Temptation #824—on sale March 2001
No way is Amanda Coppersmith going to let
The Wedding Ring rope her into marriage. But no matter
how clever she is, Nick is one step ahead of her...

*"Pamela Burford creates the
memorable characters readers love!"*
—The Literary Times

You're not going to believe this offer!

In October and November 2000, buy any two Harlequin or Silhouette books and save $10.00 off future purchases, or buy any three and save $20.00 off future purchases!

Just fill out this form and attach 2 proofs of purchase (cash register receipts) from October and November 2000 books and Harlequin will send you a coupon booklet worth a total savings of $10.00 off future purchases of Harlequin and Silhouette books in 2001. Send us 3 proofs of purchase and we will send you a coupon booklet worth a total savings of $20.00 off future purchases.

Saving money has never been this easy.

I accept your offer! Please send me a coupon booklet:

Name: _____

Address: _____ City: _____

State/Prov.: _____ Zip/Postal Code: _____

Optional Survey!

In a typical month, how many Harlequin or Silhouette books would you buy <u>new</u> at retail stores?

☐ Less than 1   ☐ 1   ☐ 2   ☐ 3 to 4   ☐ 5+

Which of the following statements best describes how you <u>buy</u> Harlequin or Silhouette books? Choose one answer only that <u>best</u> describes you.

☐ I am a regular buyer and reader
☐ I am a regular reader but buy only occasionally
☐ I only buy and read for specific times of the year, e.g. vacations
☐ I subscribe through Reader Service but also buy at retail stores
☐ I mainly borrow and buy only occasionally
☐ I am an occasional buyer and reader

Which of the following statements best describes how you <u>choose</u> the Harlequin and Silhouette series books you buy <u>new</u> at retail stores? By "series," we mean books within a particular line, such as *Harlequin PRESENTS* or *Silhouette SPECIAL EDITION*. Choose one answer only that <u>best</u> describes you.

☐ I only buy books from my favorite series
☐ I generally buy books from my favorite series but also buy books from other series on occasion
☐ I buy some books from my favorite series but also buy from many other series regularly
☐ I buy all types of books depending on my mood and what I find interesting and have no favorite series

Please send this form, along with your cash register receipts as proofs of purchase, to:
In the U.S.: Harlequin Books, P.O. Box 9057, Buffalo, NY 14269
In Canada: Harlequin Books, P.O. Box 622, Fort Erie, Ontario L2A 5X3
(Allow 4-6 weeks for delivery) Offer expires December 31, 2000.

PHQ4002

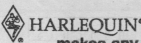